FRONTIER'S END

RYAN KIRK

❀ Created with Vellum

For Jim S.

1

———

"I'm sure you've had worse ideas," Elzeth said, "but none come immediately to mind."

Tomas grunted softly as he looked through the eyepiece of his looking glass. "You say that every time."

"Doesn't make me wrong."

The sagani lapsed into silence as Tomas studied the scene. He was prone, hidden in thick bushes across a clear lake from a new settlement. The pounding of hammers and the cutting of long saws echoed over the crystalline water, and Tomas watched the builders with a curious eye.

Even from a distance, Tomas felt the camaraderie the settlement enjoyed. As soon as one man finished framing a wall, he turned to help another. A woman brought a jug of water from the nearby stream, offering refreshment. Though sweat stained the backs of most shirts, the men and women smiled to one another as they passed.

When they finished, it wouldn't just be a town. It would be their home. Hells, it already was, even if the houses were unfinished.

They'd chosen an idyllic location. The forests were thick

with oak and maple, and the lake and nearby streams provided plenty of fish. Tomas couldn't turn around without spotting a deer. It was a plentiful land. The location wasn't the farthest west Tomas had traveled, but it was farther than most. They'd have a decade or two of peace before the flood of humanity marching across the nation reached them.

Hopefully by then, the world would be a much different place.

Tomas let the looking glass drift left and right. Only the outskirts of the town were visible through the trees. They'd wisely decided to build away from the water, unsure how high or low it would rise and fall throughout the seasons and the years. But Tomas could see enough, and he dared not approach closer until he knew more.

The winter had been the hardest he'd ever endured. Temperatures had been cold enough to freeze eyelids shut. Sharp winds tore through clothes as though his layers of protection were nothing more than an illusion. Animals had become almost impossible to track in the blowing, drifting snow. And through it all, almost no shelter to be found anywhere.

He'd become used to being pursued over the years, but nothing could have prepared him for the hunt the massacre at Chesterton had launched. As Ghosthands had promised, the story had run in every paper in the country. For a month or more, Tomas' name had been on everyone's lips, and his likeness on every street corner. Even now, half a year later, towns were as dangerous as battlefields had been during the war.

At any other point in his life, Tomas would have sounded the retreat. He would have fled to the mountains to the west and maybe even farther. The risk of remaining near others was too great, and the reward too little.

But Chesterton had been a turning point for him, too.

Fate had thrown him up against the church for years, always nudging him toward greater action. For all those years he'd struggled against it, satisfied with winning one small battle after another. But Ghosthands and Narkissa had sealed his fate as firmly as the day he'd made his pact with Elzeth. He couldn't let the church continue as it had. And if the stories he heard were any indication, he didn't have much time.

So he'd risked entering towns that wanted him dead. He listened to rumors and whispers, and he braved the coldest winter anyone alive could remember. The bitter conditions had forced him to steal to stay alive, but he'd survived.

All to end up here.

"You notice anything?" Elzeth asked.

"Not yet, but it hasn't been that long."

Elzeth didn't reply, but Tomas felt the sagani's doubt alongside his own. Tomas was certain this place was the source of all the rumors he'd followed, but the important question remained: were the rumors true?

The morning was early yet, and Tomas had nothing but time, so he watched and waited. The pace of the builders wasn't hurried, but there was an energy to their motions Tomas could sense from across the lake. The work was hard, but they were excited to complete it.

Hours passed before he spotted the sign he sought. One of the builders working on a wall had a small seizure right as Tomas had the looking glass on him. The hammer dropped from his hand and he spun in a full circle, his motions erratic. The episode lasted for no more than a few seconds, and when it was over the man looked around in a daze. Tomas' heart beat faster, as it always did at the sight.

That same future would be his before long. He didn't

know when the day would come, but he didn't take the time remaining to him for granted.

He kept his glass trained on the man, who picked up his hammer and looked around sheepishly.

The telling moments came just a few seconds later. Others, who'd been beyond the narrow focus of the looking glass, rushed toward the builder. They encircled him, the looks on their faces easy to decipher. They were concerned for their friend. And there was something else, a shared fear they tried to hide behind reassuring smiles.

The same fear Tomas had lived with every day since he'd become a host.

Tomas let the glass drop, then slowly collapsed it and stowed it in his pack. "What do you think?"

"Still hard to believe," Elzeth said.

"True enough, though it seems like it had to happen eventually, right?"

"I suppose." Elzeth paused. "You sure you want to get them involved?"

Tomas frowned. "Why wouldn't I?"

"It looks like they've got a pretty peaceful place over there. No walls, and if you didn't notice, no swords or weapons, either. And they chose a place where they won't run into any trouble for years to come. But if you so much as step foot inside there, their whole future is in jeopardy."

It wasn't that the thought hadn't occurred to Tomas, but he'd forced himself not to let his attention linger on it. Despite his best efforts, he brought chaos wherever he traveled, and his motives today weren't exactly altruistic. "We need allies."

"But if they're out here, looking for some sense of peace, you won't find allies. Even if they share some sense of your purpose, they wouldn't be here if they wanted to fight."

Tomas rolled onto his back and stared at the tree branches as they rustled in the breeze. Elzeth was probably right. He hadn't expected such a sense of peace.

But perhaps it was only an illusion. They'd only seen the outskirts of the town. Maybe there was more to it than they suspected. Still, even if what they'd seen was a true indication of the town's nature, Tomas couldn't just turn around. Not after all he'd been through to get here.

"I have to know," Tomas said.

Elzeth didn't reply, but Tomas felt the sagani's assent. Their arrival might send the town into chaos, but at least that would be an answer.

Tomas stood. Though the town was only about a thousand feet across the lake from him, it would take at least a mile of walking to reach it. He backed away from the shore and into the comforting embrace of the forest, well hidden from any casual glances the townspeople might throw his direction.

The day was almost as idyllic as the location. Brutal as the winter had been, it had at least been short-lived. Spring had moved in early this year, and the land was as green as Tomas had ever seen it. After so long looking over his shoulder, Tomas reveled in the opportunity to enjoy a leisurely stroll.

He'd rounded the end of the lake and was approaching the new town when he smelled the other man, the soft scent of soap carried downwind on the breeze. Tomas considered for a moment, then proceeded carelessly. He stepped on twigs and brushed loudly past branches.

The sound attracted his company. Less than a minute later he heard the unmistakable sound of a bow being drawn.

Tomas held up his hands and looked in the direction the

sound had come from. A young man stood there, bow in hand, arrow aimed at Tomas' chest. He looked angry. His nostrils flared and fire danced in his eyes.

"You have one minute to tell me who you are and why you're here," he said. "And if I don't like the answer, that's the last step you'll ever take."

2

———

"Name's Tomas, and I'm here because I've been hearing rumors about this place for months now. Figured I'd see it with my own eyes."

The young man's eyes narrowed. "Tomas? As in, *the* Tomas?"

"That's what people keep telling me."

"You don't look like him."

Tomas looked down at himself. "You were expecting something different?"

He got the feeling he'd said the wrong thing, because the young man fixed him with a suspicious glare that didn't bode well for Tomas' immediate future. A moment later, Tomas' growing fear was confirmed. The man pulled back on the bowstring and brought it to his cheek.

"Can't say I trust you, friend. But if you are him, then this shouldn't be a problem." He launched the arrow.

Without the warning, the arrow might have killed Tomas. The distance was too close to dodge, even with Tomas' quick reactions. But Tomas heard the threat in the archer's voice, and Elzeth flared to life within him. His sharp gaze caught the first relaxing of the young man's fingers, and he stepped to the side.

The arrow passed to his left, and Tomas sprinted forward. He didn't intend to wait around for the archer to try again.

The archer reacted faster than Tomas expected. With impossible speed, he nocked another arrow and drew the bow again. But Tomas was too close now. He slapped the bow aside with the back of his hand as the archer fired again, then followed the deflection with an uppercut from his other hand.

The young man avoided the punch, proving Tomas' suspicion he fought a host.

It didn't matter, though. Tomas was close, and though the boy had speed and a fair amount of natural aptitude, Tomas' years of training and experience still won the day. The fight ended just as quickly as it had started. Tomas stood over the young man, bow in hand. "Now do you believe me?" He extended his free hand.

The young man took it. "No, but you're definitely one of us, which is good enough for now. I can take you to the mayor." He paused, suddenly sheepish. "Name's Ross, by the way."

"Still Tomas. Pleasure to meet you," Tomas said dryly.

Ross' cheeks flushed. "Yeah. Same."

Tomas handed Ross his bow and waited while the young man retrieved his arrows. Then they started toward the town, Ross in the lead. Whatever worry had first motivated him to fire on a stranger was gone. He turned his back on Tomas as if they were long-lost friends hiking through the woods together.

"How long have you been here?" Tomas asked.

"Coming up on a year," Ross answered. "I got here last summer."

"How long you been a host?" That was a question he didn't dare ask anywhere else in the world, but here it seemed an easy one to ask.

"About twice that. Had an accident out hunting and a sagani saved my life. The rest, as they say, is history."

"Mind if I ask what brought you out here?"

Ross gave a bitter laugh. "Same as what brings everyone out here. I had a girl back home I was hoping to marry. My parents had a shop that was doing well. Life was good. But I couldn't hide the fact I was a host for long, especially as I was getting used to the new strength. Church was making life impossible for hosts and anyone who befriended them. Parents were recent converts, and they kicked me out of the house when they found out. Claimed they didn't want to share a home with a monster. The girl was even worse. So I took all the money I had and wandered west. Never could stay in a place for too long, though, afraid that someone would find out. Eventually I started hearing rumors about this town, and here I am."

Ross turned back to look at him. "What about you? If you are who you say you are, then you're in a whole mess of trouble."

Tomas debated how much he should say. With the number of questions he had about the town, he figured it was best to keep his cards close to his chest to start. He chose to share some of the truth. "I'm looking to make things better for hosts. When I first heard about this place, I thought I might find some allies here."

Ross might have been quick to attack, but he was no fool. "What kind of allies you looking for?"

"I suppose that depends on what your mayor says when I speak to him."

"Her," Ross corrected. He slowed to a stop. "You here to find fighters?"

Tomas winced. It was the one question he really didn't want to answer. But now that it was out in the open, he felt like he had no choice. "Maybe. Don't really want to say much until I talk with your mayor."

They reached the outskirts of the town, not far from the place Tomas had been observing through his looking glass less than an hour ago. The sounds of construction were louder here, the energy more palpable. Ross led him through, nodding his greetings to others as they passed.

Tomas attracted attention, as any stranger in a town this small would, but less than he expected. They might have heard his name out here, but the church and marshals hadn't been through with piles of posters, so his anonymity held for the moment. With Ross as his escort, no one seemed too concerned about his presence. Tomas returned nods to those who offered them, but mostly he let his gaze wander around.

The first and most obvious detail he noticed about the town was that everything looked new. He couldn't find any peeling paint, faded signs, or broken windows no matter how hard he searched. He'd suspected the town wasn't old, but everything he saw led him to guess the whole place hadn't been established more than three or four years ago.

For a tiny town, though, the streets were almost as busy as a city. It seemed everyone was out of their homes, running errands or working on projects. Everyone they passed walked with a sense of purpose. It felt surreal.

Ross navigated around the construction projects until he came to a small house. An old woman sat in a rocking chair, watching the activity with a wary eye. Ross bowed as he stopped in front of the porch. "Ms. Ulva, this here man claims to be Tomas. Says he wants to speak to you."

It took a moment for Tomas to realize he was looking at the mayor of this town. Skin hung from her bones and her back looked as though it was permanently bent forward. Tomas was a terrible judge of age, but he wouldn't have been surprised if the woman in front of him had personally seen over ninety years of history. She might have been the oldest person he'd ever met.

How in the three hells had she become mayor of this town? Was Ross playing some sort of trick?

Then a mosquito made the unfortunate decision to approach Ulva. Her hand snapped out and she caught the bug, squishing it between thumb and forefinger. She looked up at him with sharp eyes that missed nothing.

Well, that explained that.

Tomas offered her a bow that would have satisfied any of his most demanding superiors in the army. She bowed her head in return. When she spoke, her voice was strong and clear. "Tomas, eh? Well, let's mosey on inside where we can talk without disturbing the peace." She turned to Ross. "Thanks for bringing him straight to me. I'd appreciate it if you keep his name quiet until I can decide if he's telling the truth."

Ross nodded, bowed, and left. Ulva glared at him as he walked away.

Then she stood from the rocking chair, rising with a strength and grace people twenty years her junior would have been jealous of. "You look like the kind of man who appreciates a good cup of tea. Do you appreciate a good cup of tea, Tomas?"

"Yes, ma'am."

"Then get on in here, and we'll see if we can settle things before your presence starts a war in this town."

3

———

Ulva stepped inside before Tomas could question her cryptic remark. He looked up and down the street, but no one paid him much attention. That, at least, was a nice change. He shrugged to himself and followed the old woman into her home.

She was hunched over a stove, warming a kettle. Tomas took off his boots and sat at a small table. After a few minutes of fussing with the water, she came over with two chipped cups and poured him tea.

"What's this about a war?" he asked.

"What war?" she asked in response.

Tomas swore to himself. The woman moved like a host, but what if her mind was already being devoured by the sagani within? Or maybe she was just succumbing to old age. "You said we should talk before my presence set off a war in town."

"As well it might."

"So—what war?"

"Between those of us who think you're a hero and those of us who don't want a thing to do with you. You're a popular topic of conversation in these parts, assuming you're the same Tomas who's the most wanted man in the country."

Tomas noted she placed herself in both possible camps. "If I was, what would you do?"

She smiled. "Probably invite you into my house for tea."

Tomas grinned. In a battle of wits, he got the impression he was completely outclassed. But he charged forward anyway. "I was hoping to speak to you about some of my plans."

Ulva cackled as though he'd told a joke. "I'm sure you were! Everyone has such grand plans. As if I don't have anything better to do than listen to you young ones tell me how you're going to change the world. I won't be around forever, you know. I've got better things to do with my time."

Tomas blinked and shook his head. If this conversation *was* a battlefield, his opponent was making all their moves under the cover of dense fog. He had no idea how to proceed. "Any suggestions here?" he asked Elzeth.

"She's more than she seems," Elzeth said. "There's something about her I can't quite place, something with her sagani I've not felt before."

Tomas sniffed the tea, then sipped it. The brew was tasty. He took another sip. He studied the mayor for a moment, debating how to ask what needed asking. After coming up with nothing useful, he defaulted to his normal tactics. He'd always found blunt, straightforward truth a useful approach. So he tried it here.

"I want your town's help to fight the church."

Ulva drank her own tea. Then she put the cup down and shook her head. "I like you. Straight and to the point. Not wasting my time. You could probably teach the people here a few things. I'll be equally straight with you. I will not do a damned thing to help you."

"Why not?"

Ulva snorted. "You even listen to yourself when you speak? No one can meaningfully fight the church, no matter how strong they are. Hells, I'm not even sure the army could at this point. Besides, I'm old enough to remember the war before the war you all fought in. As tempting as violence is, it solves nothing."

Her words left a cold feeling in the pit of his stomach. He clenched his fists. "Do you know what they've done?"

"Horrible things, I'm sure. But it doesn't change the facts. Your own life is proof enough of that. What good did the Chesterton Massacre accomplish? You didn't hurt the church, even though you killed dozens of them. From what I hear, their ranks are swelling with members, and more people want to outlaw hosts than ever before. The whole damn west is flooded with believers out to start some sort of holy land."

The quiet question was like a slap to the face. And her description of the consequences was accurate. Ghosthands' plan had proved to be nearly prophetic. "I never wanted a massacre."

Ulva spread out her hands. "I've never wanted a massacre, either, and I've found it surprisingly easy to not commit one. And I dare say I've done less to help the church in the past year than you have."

"I was forced to."

"I very much doubt that. Perhaps it felt that way, but it was your choice. You chose poorly."

Tomas gritted his teeth. He'd hoped that if there was any place in the world he would find understanding, it would be here. A town full of hosts, all escaping the persecution of the church. If he found no allies here, he'd find them nowhere. But Chesterton damned him, even in their eyes.

With a conscious effort he released his anger. It did him no good. All that this meant was that he would have to find a different way. There was nothing for it.

He finished his tea, then stood up and bowed. Despite Ulva's decision, he respected what she attempted here and hoped it succeeded. "I'm sorry I've wasted your time. I'll be on my way."

"Oh, sit down! You're wound up tighter than a new watch."

Tomas frowned, well and truly confused. "But you said you wouldn't help me."

"And if I was the only person in this town whose opinion mattered, you could be on your way. But I'm not, and you also happened to have the good fortune, if one could call it that, to run into Ross, who I'm sure is running as fast as he can to go find Hardin."

"You told him to keep it quiet."

Ulva gave a bitter snort. "You think I run this town with an iron fist? All I ever wanted to do was start a refuge, a place where I and a few like-minded folks could escape the church. I never set out to start a town, and I sure as hells didn't plan on running one. What authority I have here is only because no one else has stepped up to lead the place."

"Ross said you were the mayor."

"They all say that. I keep trying to tell them to leave me alone, but it seems I was voted in without my consent."

Tomas scratched his head. "So...?"

"So sit down, and if you're capable of it, we can talk like civilized adults before Hardin and his crew show up. Maybe you'll at least have the good sense to listen to me."

Tomas sat back down, and Ulva poured him another cup of tea. She continued. "Perhaps it's best if you tell me what you know about this town, what your plan is for dealing with the church, and how you think we'll help."

Tomas sipped at the tea and collected his thoughts. "Well, I don't know much about this town. Only that it serves as a refuge for hosts, a place beyond the church's vision. I have no specific plan for fighting the church yet, but I have an idea to seek out and destroy some of their research facilities. I can't do it alone."

"Do you even know this town's name?"

Tomas admitted he didn't. "Never had one in any of the rumors I heard."

"Jonasson."

"Nice name."

"Thanks. Came up with it myself. But that's beside the point. You clearly don't know much about us, so how about your plan for the church? Why their research facilities? Why not assassinate the Holy Father?"

"Pointless," Tomas answered. "There will just be another one, and it will only make a martyr of the current one. I'm not a fool that believes I can destroy the church. But they're trying to wipe out hosts and sagani alike, and their researchers will go to any lengths to succeed. Have you heard any of the rumors of a new weapon?"

Ulva shrugged. "I hear rumors of all sorts of things. Doesn't mean I believe any of them."

"I do, and I mean to put a stop to their work, or at least delay it for as many years as I can."

"And you figured you might find allies here?"

There was more bitterness in the question than Tomas expected. "Can you blame me? As far as I know, this is the only place in the nation that welcomes hosts."

She stared into her cup. "Might as well let you know what's what around here. I started Jonasson about three years ago, never intending for it to be an actual town. A lot more people found their way here than I ever expected. But it's been good, and I'd like to think we've served as a refuge for many who had nowhere else to turn. We had our first weddings here last year, and this summer we're expecting our first children."

"Congratulations."

"Thank you." Ulva's gaze hardened as she met his eyes. "I never wanted this place to be anything more than a refuge. I lost my husband in the first war and my boys in the second. There's no reason for fighting, so far as I can see. Just causes more fighting down the road. But not everyone sees it that way."

"Hardin?" Tomas guessed.

Ulva nodded. "The one and only."

"What's his story?"

"Wife fought in the unnamed units during the war. They met on the battlefield and fell in love. Jump forward a few years and she started going mad. Ended up killing herself before it took her dignity. A sad story, made worse because they spent the last years of their lives together on the run from the church. From what I hear, it wasn't pleasant."

"He became a host just to get revenge?"

"Sure did. People tell me he's a great swordsman, and I can tell you he's as clever as they come. He came here two years ago, on the run after hitting an army caravan."

"Why'd you let him in, if you're so against violence?"

She stared out the window of her home, and Tomas thought she was searching for something. "It's a question I've gone back and forth on dozens of times. The short version is that I wanted this to be a place that welcomed people no matter what their past was like. I told Hardin he was welcome so long as he kept out of trouble."

"Did he?"

She scoffed. "Recruited a few of the younger hosts and hit another supply wagon less than three months after moving in. He and I argued then, and he left. Set up a place about a mile north."

"Doesn't seem far enough."

"It did at the time. But the town has grown, and Hardin's enclave has as well. Now it's only a half mile away from the outskirts of town, and the families of each are close enough we might as well be a single town."

"Why'd you let him?"

"What was I going to do? I've already told you I have no appetite for violence and never sought to run this town. For the most part, I let him be and he leaves me be. Don't think that'll happen with you around, though. He'll want you."

Tomas finished this cup of tea. "It sounds like he might be the one I want to speak to, anyway."

"For what you're planning, you're probably right. Might you permit an old lady one suggestion, though?"

Tomas found he didn't have much interest, but the mayor had been kind enough to him, and he typically found the wisdom of his elders worth considering. "Of course."

"Leave this place. Leave now and never return. When I look at you, I'm reminded of Hardin. You're both polite and respectful, but stubborn as mules. You're so convinced about the rightness of what you're doing you never really stop to think."

"I—"

Ulva barreled through his objection. "Think about this, then. If you drag Hardin into whatever schemes you plan, you'll be dragging this town right along. And most people here don't want the first thing to do with you. They came here to escape the church, maybe even forget about it in time. Not fight it. You work with Hardin, and the consequences will spread far beyond just the two of you. You'll be risking the happiness of no small number of families. Families with hosts, the very people you claim you're protecting. It would be a monstrous deed."

Tomas swallowed the sudden lump in his throat.

Her words struck true, and they echoed Ghosthands' accusations.

He'd debated those questions with Elzeth endlessly over the long winter nights, and they still weren't any closer to an answer.

Was he as much a monster as the church?

He didn't have any answer today, but Ulva was right. If he and Hardin did work together, the church wouldn't see any difference between Jonasson and Hardin's enclave. But if he left, it felt like surrendering to the church. There were allies here! He couldn't just abandon the possibilities.

In the end, Ulva's request came too late. Outside, Tomas heard horses galloping down the street toward the house. Ulva's shoulders slumped in surrender.

Hardin had arrived.

4

"Looks like you'll get to meet the man himself," Ulva muttered.

Tomas glanced from the window back to the mayor. This meeting had left him unsettled and more uncertain than he'd been in months. The church's actions cried out for justice, but at what cost? Was he willing to sacrifice this oasis of peace? He stood and bowed to the mayor, deeper than before. "I'll keep your warning in mind, truly."

Ulva didn't look satisfied with the promise, but she swallowed her disappointment and nodded. "See that you do."

Tomas stepped from the house in time to see three riders pull their mounts to a stop. The two on the flanks were younger men. Hardin rode between them. Though they'd never met, there could be no doubt. He looked to be several years older than Tomas. If he'd become a host after the war, it stood to reason they were of almost the same age.

A presence surrounded him, though. A powerful air of command Tomas hadn't felt from anyone since leaving the service. Hardin dismounted in one smooth motion. He stood a full head and then some above Tomas, with arms that looked strong enough to squeeze the life out of a bear in a wrestling match.

The other two riders also dismounted, and Hardin handed the reins of his horse to one of them. The young man looked damn near ecstatic to be honored with the task. The other young man looked at Tomas the way believers stared at portraits of the Holy Father. Tomas' eyes narrowed at the sight. He sought allies. Not fanatics.

Hardin wasted no time in striding forward. He bowed deeply. "My name is Hardin, and it's a pleasure to welcome you."

Tomas returned the bow. "Tomas, and thank you for the hospitality."

Behind Hardin, a crowd began to gather. Workers put down their tools, and conversations ceased as heads turned. Tomas sighed. The anonymity had been nice while it lasted.

"Are you him?" Hardin asked.

"I am."

Hardin drew his sword. "Please don't take offense, but I must know for sure."

Behind Tomas, Ulva stepped onto her porch. "Just what do you think you're doing, Hardin? You agreed you'd bare no steel on these streets short of imminent danger."

Indecision flickered across Hardin's face, but it settled quickly. "This will take but a moment, and if he is who he says he is, there will be no bloodshed."

"He is who he says he is. Now get, before you do something we all regret."

Tomas saw the bind the two of them had placed themselves in. Ulva couldn't permit violence in her town because the moment she did, it would open the door for more. But Hardin couldn't back down from his challenge, not with his fanatic loyalists behind him. The crowd that had gathered was so silent it was as if they were all holding their breath at once.

The solution was simple enough. Tomas turned and bowed to Ulva. "Thank you, both for the warm welcome and the tea. I think it best I be going for now, but I hope our paths cross again. Until they do, I wish you the best of luck. What you do here is a great thing."

Then he turned to Hardin. "Agreed, but not here. Ms. Ulva has been more than hospitable, and I'll respect her rules."

It gave Hardin a way out that saved face. He gave Tomas a slight nod, acknowledging the opportunity. Then he bowed formally and sheathed his sword. "Very well. Will you walk with me?"

"Of course."

Hardin pointed them north, in the direction he had come from. Tomas followed, and the two men trailed a respectful distance behind, bringing the horses with them.

"How much did Ulva tell you?" Hardin asked.

"She didn't want the two of us to meet. She feared that if we made common cause, it would only bring ruin upon the settlement."

"And you? What do you think?"

"I don't know nearly enough to make a wise choice. Though from what little I have seen, this is someplace special, someplace worth protecting. I fear she may be right."

"We are of like minds, then. I often feel just as torn."

Tomas raised an eyebrow. "Ulva would have me believe you spared no thought to the well-being of the settlement."

Hardin grimaced. "There is always a balance between competing values. Ulva and I share many, but we weight them differently. It would be unfair to say I'm not concerned with the fate of the settlement, but I balance it against other considerations."

Hardin impressed Tomas. From the short conversation with Ulva, he'd expected someone stubborn and rough. But Hardin struck him as articulate and thoughtful.

By the time they left the outskirts of the settlement, it was just the four of them. Ulva's townspeople had decided whatever drama might unfold wasn't worth the time and had trickled back to their work. Tomas had little doubt they'd hear about the events to come one way or the other.

Hardin led them to a clearing in the trees where the brush had been cut back and the dirt and grass trampled flat. He gestured around the space. "Is this sufficient?"

Tomas could find no fault and nodded. "We don't really have to do this. I'm not keen to draw my sword against another host, even if it is to prove I speak true."

"Understood. But your arrival changes everything, and I would be a poor leader if I didn't test your claim. Too much hinges on your identity."

Tomas drew his sword. "Fair enough." He hadn't had a good fight in over a month, but he'd trained diligently. His defeat at Ghosthands' blade colored almost every waking thought, and he desperately sought a way to break free of the inevitable conclusion that would result if they crossed swords again.

Perhaps part of his answer was here. He couldn't beat Ghosthands on his own, but Hardin seemed strong. He could fall alone, or stand together.

This exchange would answer that question.

He attacked with a fast overhand cut. Hardin avoided it easily, and Elzeth burned as the duel began in earnest. Their blades whispered through the air as they danced around one another.

It was over in three passes. Hardin stopped his sword less than an inch away from Tomas' neck, and Tomas froze his almost the same distance away from Hardin's chest.

Hardin grunted, then stepped back. Tomas did the same. They sheathed their weapons, and Hardin studied him. "How close were you to unity?"

"Close. Had a bit more to give, first."

Hardin nodded. Tomas glanced over to the two young men, whose wide eyes gave away their astonishment. He'd impressed them, at least.

Hardin saw the direction of Tomas' gaze, glanced over at his aides, and chuckled. "They've never seen anyone earn a draw against me."

"You're almost as good as anyone I've ever met," Tomas said. "You were in the army?"

"First squad, first army. It true you served in the unnamed units?"

"I did. Worked with the first army once or twice. Third squad, though." Tomas studied Hardin in a new light. First squad was reserved for the best swords in each army, and first army was the best of them all. Hardin would have been one of the best swords in the country, and that was before he became a host.

A powerful ally, indeed.

"She tell you Allie was in the unnamed units, too?"

Tomas admitted that Ulva had.

"That was how we met. She wasn't the best sword, not even in her unit, but there was a grace to her style that I've never seen before or since." Hardin's eyes were unfocused, lost in memories of the past. He shook his head gently and returned his attention to Tomas. "To be honest, I'd expected you to be a bit stronger."

Tomas took no insult, because none was intended. "I've always only been good enough to survive. Mostly I'm just always in the wrong place at the wrong time, at least if you're asking anyone in the church."

"I don't think it's just that. It's that you don't stand for what others meekly accept. I've heard enough of the stories." Hardin nodded, then straightened as he clearly came to a decision. "Well, maybe your streak ends here. I have the feeling you're in the right place at exactly the right time."

The words heartened Tomas more than he expected. Hardin turned, gesturing for him to follow. "No need to commit to anything yet, but let me show you my home. We can talk a bit and decide from there."

Tomas followed Hardin out of the clearing, the young men eagerly trailing behind the two warriors, horses in tow.

"How long have you been a host, Tomas?" Hardin asked.

"I met Elzeth the first year of the war."

Hardin whistled softly. "I'd heard you'd been a host for a long time. But that's a really long time." There was a note of pain in his voice that Tomas guessed was for his wife. It had to be hard, talking with a man who'd been a host for so many years and still walked on this side of the gates. "No tics?"

"None that I've seen. You're welcome to search for them, though. I always fear I won't notice them when they happen."

"I will."

Tomas sensed that Hardin had more questions, but then they reached the outskirts of another settlement. Hardin opened his arms wide. "Welcome to Alliston."

Hardin caught Tomas' look and shrugged. "Can't blame me for naming it after my wife. Ulva named Jonasson after her husband."

Tomas supposed he couldn't.

Hardin waved him forward. "Come on in. Let me show you the place where I hope we can change the world."

5

———

Tomas' first thought, when he looked at Alliston, was that it was a distorted mirror's image of Jonasson. There were many similarities, though each was twisted by Hardin's competing priorities.

Alliston only contained about a dozen houses, but more were in the process of being raised. As before, the air was filled with the sounds of saws and hammers. Citizens moved briskly from one task to the next, and Tomas felt the same sense of purpose he had in Ulva's settlement.

The differences were obvious, though. The beginnings of a wall were being built, a construction project that looked as though it occupied about half the citizens. Swords were everywhere. Some wore them at their side as they worked while others settled for keeping them close at hand. Tomas felt like he saw more swords than people.

He noted the differences in the citizens of the two settlements. He'd been impressed by the wide range of people Jonasson had attracted. There'd been hosts young and old, and it looked as though many had brought their families with them. That wasn't the case here.

Alliston was mostly younger men. What women were here looked just as dangerous, and most people had an aura about them that made Tomas suspect they were former soldiers. He didn't see any families here. The atmosphere here was different, yet it felt eerily familiar. It took him a moment to articulate why.

Alliston felt more like a permanent military camp than a settlement.

Hardin took him on a brief tour, although Tomas noted there were no introductions made. Eventually, they ended up at a small home that looked for all the world like Ulva's. The two hosts stepped inside while the other two young men took the horses to the stables. Tomas gestured after them. "Don't you worry word of my arrival will spread?"

Hardin shook his head. "I trust them as much as I would trust anyone in this town, which is to say, with my life. I asked them not to speak of your arrival until you and I could talk in private, and they'll obey, no matter how tempted they might be. You can't have a fighting force without that basic trust."

They sat down at a table that appeared to be the exact same one Tomas had just stood up from in the neighboring settlement. He couldn't help but let the corner of his lips turn up in a smile at the sight. Likely everyone was working from the same plans. Or the tables had been made by the same person.

"So, that's your idea? To start a settlement of hosts that doubles as some sort of army unit?" Tomas asked.

"Would you believe me if I told you no?"

Tomas shrugged. "All I know is what little Ulva told me, and I'm usually skeptical until I observe something with my own eyes."

Hardin looked off in the distance for a moment before

answering. "The truth is, Ulva and I mostly have the same goals. Like her, my goal is to build a settlement, and someday a town, that will welcome everyone, including hosts, and provide a safe place for them to live."

Tomas narrowed his eyes. "From what I see, this place feels more like a military camp than a welcoming settlement."

Hardin didn't dispute the observation. "By necessity, unfortunately. Let me ask you this: What do you believe will happen to Jonasson? What does it look like, five or ten years from now, if I don't do something?"

Tomas knew what he believed. "The church destroys it."

A brief look of relief passed across Hardin's face at their shared understanding. "Agreed. Though Ulva doesn't believe me when I tell her this, I respect her pacifism. I wish we lived in a world in which her beliefs were sufficient, and to tell you the truth, I'll keep fighting to help make that world a reality. I'll fight so that she doesn't have to."

A vague idea was forming in Tomas' head, an understanding that hadn't quite assumed definite shape. He was left with the impression Hardin had thought longer and harder about the future of these towns than even Ulva, but the details of his plans still eluded Tomas. "But what about the attacks on caravans? You're just risking more attention, doing that."

"It's all the same answer. I attack the caravans because we're fighting a war, even if Ulva hasn't realized it. Our enemy has far more resources than we do. By robbing those caravans, we're absorbing their resources and denying those same resources to the church."

"At tremendous risk to both your settlements."

"Risk, yes. Tremendous? I'm not so sure. We do all we can to reduce the risk of our raids. We rarely hit the same routes or attack in the same manner. I don't think the church is on to us yet. But even if they were, the overall problem remains the same. If we do nothing, we're overwhelmed within ten years at most. We need to take risks now to survive tomorrow."

"Then why build so close to Ulva? If you're as serious about mitigating risks as you say, why not be someplace else? You'll wrap them up in this."

"They *are* wrapped up in this, they just refuse to see it. Again, Ulva's only looking at what is. She's not looking at what will be. If I am not near, in less than a decade, the church comes by and wipes them out, and they'll be in no position to do anything about it. With Alliston nearby, they'll have a fighting force of hosts and walls they can retreat to if the worst comes to pass." He shrugged. "And I'll also admit that scale matters. I couldn't have built Alliston as quickly as I did without help from hosts in Ulva's settlement, and I've returned aid in plenty of ways. It's been a beneficial arrangement."

Tomas leaned back in his chair and finally allowed his own skepticism to slip. Hardin was a far different man than he'd expected to meet after his talk with Ulva. Which raised one last question. "That all seems reasonable enough to me. If I were to repeat this all to Ulva, what would she say?"

Hardin grinned. "Now that's a wonderful question, and easy enough to answer. She would tell you I'm wrong."

Tomas chuckled. "You've had this debate before?"

"More times than I can count. I try to meet her for tea at least once a week, and for almost a year, we argued the same things every day. Our differences don't come from our goals, but from how we view the world and the church. Because we can't agree on that, we can't agree on anything that comes after. Ulva would tell you the church is not as despicable as I would. She would tell you that the vast majority of churchgoers are good and decent people who would never stoop so low as to wipe out a whole town of peaceful people. She believes that it's only because of the violence we commit that we bring violence into our lives."

The night of the Chesterton Massacre ran through Tomas' mind. How a town had hung two innocents, including their own priest. He didn't believe that any of Chesterton's residents had been evil. That kind of thinking had always struck him as being too simple, too easy a way out. All people held both good and evil in their hearts, but that didn't make them one or the other. Good people could commit unspeakable atrocities, just as evil people could do good.

"Say I agree with you. What's your plan?"

"Probably not as specific as you'd like. I just know that I want to see Ulva's endeavor succeed. For now, we steal resources away from the church, plus recruit and train hosts who are willing to fight. I'll build Alliston and keep an eye on the church so that when they decide to move against us, we're ready. I know that I'll never be able to stand up to the might of the whole church. My goal, such as it is, is to make this place too expensive for them to want to take."

Tomas nodded along. Hardin had given him a lot to think about.

Hardin seemed to have a window into his thoughts. "It's quite a bit to take in, so I'll not ask you to decide anything now. But may I ask a question of my own?"

Tomas nodded.

"By now, you're as much myth as you are person, especially among hosts. I don't mind taking in criminals, because the church forces that upon many of us. But I do want to know about you. I want to hear your story from your own lips. And I want to know why you're here."

So Tomas told his story, from his time in the unnamed units all the way to the present. Hardin listened silently, giving Tomas' story his full attention. When Tomas finished, Hardin only had one question. "What did you hope to accomplish by coming here?"

"You've heard the rumors of the weapons?"

Hardin nodded.

"I don't know what's true and what's not. But I get the sense the church is making their move. The only way I can think to hit them, in any way that hurts, is to hit their research laboratories. It might not stop their weapon development, or whatever else they're working on, but it'll hurt them."

Hardin thought on the proposal for a few minutes. Then he extended his hand. "I'm more than willing to help, if you'd like."

Tomas took the extended hand and shook it, silently apologizing to Ulva.

The deal done, Hardin stood up. "I'll introduce you to everyone soon, but I think there's something you'll want to see, first. I think you'll be impressed."

6

On the way out the door, Hardin and Tomas encountered a group of young men who had been searching for Hardin. Tomas hung back while Hardin spoke with the group, answering questions about the order he wanted a few of their projects completed in. Again, Tomas was reminded of a military camp. The young men hadn't come for a discussion, but for orders.

After a minute the group departed, eager to start their next project. Hardin led Tomas north, roughly paralleling the shore of the lake. They skirted around the half-constructed walls and were soon surrounded by enormous oaks.

"Do people always come to you for orders?" Tomas asked.

Hardin grimaced. "More than I'd like. I've set up a command structure not that different from an army's, so only the most important decisions should make it to me, but people are nervous they'll make a mistake, so I end up with most of the decisions anyway."

"How do you see Alliston being governed in the future?"

"Well, for now, the place is small enough that it's pretty simple. Most decisions, I just make. If something comes up that I'm not sure about, or if it feels like a decision that requires consent, then I'll call the town together and we'll discuss it. So far it's worked out well. Hopefully by the time it doesn't, I'll be dead and not need to worry about it." Hardin's cheerful mood faded. "Honestly, though, I'd like to see Alliston and Jonasson become one, and I think the leadership should come from over there. It's better we take orders than think we're in charge."

"Smart." Tomas looked around. "Don't suppose you're going to tell me where we're going, are you?"

"Figured I'd keep it a surprise."

Elzeth chimed in, the first time the sagani had stirred in a while. "He's taking you to a nexus."

"How close?"

"Not that far now."

Hardin led him on for almost another mile, to a rock outcropping with dark stone that looked like it had bubbled up from the ground millions of years ago. A familiar blue glow emanated from within. "You're building near a nexus," Tomas said.

Hardin nodded. "You've seen these before?"

"Several times."

They stepped into the cave, though it barely deserved the name. The whole space was smaller than Hardin's house. The nexus sat peacefully near the back of the cave, the uncut crystal glowing with the power Tomas wished he better understood. This was the most easily accessible nexus he'd come across, and the first time he'd come across one not guarded by monsters, whether they be human or sagani.

"Don't touch it," Hardin said. "The young man who

discovered it did so and died a few moments later. Still don't know why."

"It separates host and sagani," Tomas said. "The sagani lives on, I think, but the host dies."

Hardin raised an eyebrow. "How'd you figure that out?"

"Touched one."

"And lived to tell about it?"

"It was a close thing." Tomas changed the subject. "You know the church wants these something fierce, right? You might as well be building your house on a pile of dynamite."

Hardin shrugged. "I'd heard. In fairness, we were building the town before we found this. Now I figure it doesn't make much difference one way or the other. They'll want us dead regardless."

Hardin impressed Tomas. The man stared, unblinking, into the future. Tomas couldn't say that about too many people. Maybe not even about himself.

A sudden urge came over him. "Want to touch it?" he asked Elzeth.

"You know *I* want to, but why would you? Every time we come into contact with those things you're risking your life."

"Because last time was different. Even for you. We still don't have a clue what these are, but every time we touch one, we learn a little more."

Elzeth considered for a while. "Your death, not mine."

The words were dismissive, but the answer wasn't. Though Elzeth wouldn't die, he was in no hurry to leave Tomas. He agreed because he believed the risk was worth it. Tomas stepped toward the nexus.

Hardin put a hand on his shoulder, holding him back. "What are you doing?"

"Touching it. But I don't intend to die."

Different emotions warred on Hardin's face, but after a moment he let go. "You always this reckless?"

Tomas snorted. "Ask the church."

He reached out and touched the glowing stone.

The wave of energy crashed over him the moment his fingertips made contact. He'd expected it, though. Against every instinct in his body, he relaxed his muscles and allowed the strength to flow through him unimpeded.

Time slowed, and Tomas saw Hardin's face twisted in amusement. Old wounds and aches washed away, and Tomas reached out for Elzeth. Unlike their first encounters with a nexus, Tomas found him without too much difficulty. It still wasn't easy, but it didn't feel as impossible as it had once had. He knew what to look for.

Sensations poured into him like water into a cup, filling him past the brim but refusing to stop. He felt as though he was caught in a spider's web, entwined in a vast network of life, impossibly complex and beautiful beyond compare.

He drifted on oceans of experience, soaking in all that he could. The whole world beckoned, and he answered its call, drifting along the web aimlessly. He floated across the surface, but it felt like there was something more, something deeper that he couldn't quite reach.

With a start, he realized he had lost track of time, that his sense of the physical world had vanished. His mind raced as he feared he'd lost the connection to his body. He sought it with a slowly growing sense of unease.

Then he found it, a mote of darkness in the middle of an ocean of light. He pulled himself toward it, fighting against invisible currents. His own mind betrayed him, longing for the peaceful eternity found within the nexus. Here, there was no doubt, no uncertainty, and no guilt. He was as innocent as the church claimed to be.

Only a whisper in the back of his mind kept him pulling toward reality, toward suffering. A soft voice, reminding him his work wasn't yet complete. He hadn't yet earned the right to rest. The darkness grew until it surrounded him.

Back in the world, he pulled his fingers away from the glowing stone, and they came away easily.

He felt *good*. Better even than after his previous contacts with nexuses. It wasn't just that the aches and pains were gone, but his thoughts were quieter than they'd been in a long while. He suspected the peace was temporary, but he welcomed it all the same. He looked up to see Hardin staring at him, eyes wide.

"What did you see?" Tomas asked.

Hardin's eyes narrowed. "What do you mean? You daintily tapped your finger against the nexus, then turned and looked at me."

Tomas grunted. It wasn't just that time passed differently, then. It was that time barely existed at all in that space.

"Elzeth?" He could still feel the sagani, but was surprised at his partner's silence.

"What?" Elzeth asked.

"You fine?"

"I need a bit. But yes, I'm fine. No need to worry."

Tomas wasn't sure he believed Elzeth, but they'd have plenty of time to talk later.

It was the nexus, though, that solidified Tomas' decision. This was the first place where he'd have uninterrupted access to one, and he didn't want to waste that opportunity. If he could understand the glowing stones, he might just have the key he needed to wage a war against the church.

Hells, he probably would have stayed anyway, but this was a nice justification.

Hardin stepped closer to the nexus, curiosity etched in every line on his face. His hand inched up, growing ever closer. Tomas reached out and put a hand on Hardin's shoulder, their positions now reversed. "I won't stop you, if that's what you really want, but in my experience, it's unwise. Every time I've seen another host touch these things, they die."

Hardin flinched as though he'd been struck. But he stood his ground, staring at the nexus with obvious desire. Tomas tried again. "Does the need come from your sagani? It pulls the creatures to it. Make sure that if this is something you do, it's your choice alone."

Hardin hesitated, hand outstretched, only a few inches away from the stone. Then his hand dropped to his side, and it looked like it was one of the hardest things he'd ever done.

They left the nexus, putting the temptation behind them. Hardin was quiet, his gaze locked on the ground before him. Tomas gave him space, welcoming the silence himself. Just this morning he'd been staring at Jonasson from across the lake, and now he'd met the mayors of two settlements and touched a nexus. It was a lot to take in.

As they neared Alliston, Hardin returned to himself. He acknowledged Tomas' respectful silence with a nod. Up ahead, they heard wooden swords sparring. "Care to take a look at our training?" Hardin asked.

"Please."

They angled toward the edge of the town, where a training ground had been cleared. A variety of practice weapons rested in stands around the perimeter, and half a dozen younger warriors were sparring and practicing their forms. Hardin stopped well short of the group so that they could observe without disrupting the routine.

Tomas liked what he saw. The techniques were of widely

varied quality, but the young woman who instructed the others knew exactly what corrections were required. Hardin noticed Tomas studying her. "Her name is Myra. She was in the army before she became a host. She's an excellent sword in her own right, but she's one of the best instructors I've ever come across. Always knows exactly what's needed. It's a rare gift."

Tomas agreed. Granted, he hadn't come across too many poor instructors in his life. Between the sword schools and the military, weak instructors were weeded out quickly. The students faced real combat and needed to be prepared. But there was a difference between a good instructor and a great one, and Myra clearly fell in the latter camp. Tomas noted the improvement in the students' techniques in just one training session.

They watched for a few minutes before there was a lull in the activity. Hardin gestured for Tomas to follow. "Come on, I'll introduce you."

They hadn't even stepped inside the training circle before they heard running footsteps from the center of the town. Hardin and Tomas turned together to see Ross, a note in his hand. He handed it to Hardin. "Just got word from one of our informants."

Hardin read it quickly. "Gather first squad at my home, please."

Ross nodded and ran off again. Tomas chuckled as he watched the young man disappear back into the settlement. The young man was putting a lot of miles on his boots today.

"Afraid introductions will have to wait," Hardin said. "We're probably going to be heading out by day's end. I didn't plan on asking you to commit to anything yet, but you're welcome to ride along with us and see what we're about."

"Might mean more trouble for you, if things go bad."

Hardin shrugged. "Things go bad for us, the amount of trouble doesn't much matter."

Tomas only needed a moment. "Not promising anything yet," Tomas said, "but I'd like to tag along, if you don't mind."

Hardin grinned. "Not at all, friend. Not at all."

7

———

Hardin's warriors organized with a speed that would have made any general envious. By the time Tomas and Hardin arrived at Hardin's house, two warriors were already present. They'd been lounging on the porch, but the moment Hardin strode into view, they leaped up as though ready for inspection. By the time Hardin had led them into his dining room and found the appropriate maps, three more had arrived. Myra was the last to show up, the sweat on her forehead evidence of the training she'd just been supervising.

Hardin introduced Tomas. "Y'all have heard of Tomas by now. He and I are still talking some things out, but he's interested in what we're doing here. He's coming along as an observer. Nothing more."

Most of Hardin's first squad looked excited at the news, but a few looked upset. Tomas didn't know if it was because they wanted more commitment from him, or if they didn't want him around at all.

Hardin didn't seem concerned. He launched straight into a description of the mission. A two-wagon caravan had just departed from a small town to the east and was heading to a new settlement to the southwest called Kimson. The informant wasn't too sure what the wagons were carrying, but the wagons had left under the cover of night.

The caravan's path was easy enough to determine. The west didn't have the complex sets of roads the eastern half of the country did, so there was only one road it could follow to the settlement, most of which passed through wide-open prairie.

Tomas asked about Kimson. Hardin shrugged. "Don't know much about it, yet. It's almost all church, and it's been quiet. Been meaning to ride that way to scout it out, but it's a fair distance, and they only got established late last summer. Haven't had time."

The briefing continued, and the squad largely ignored Tomas as they fell into what was clearly a familiar practice. Hardin owned good maps, with topographic features easily identifiable. He and his warriors discussed possible ambush points, debating the advantages and disadvantages of each. After a few quick minutes of discussion, it was clear there were two locations that were far superior to any other. One would require a hard ride, the other a slightly easier one.

All eyes turned to Hardin as the last arguments were made.

He only debated for a few moments. He stabbed his finger down on the map. "We'll hit them here. It'll be the harder ride, but it's farther away from Alliston. The lay of the land means we'll also have to run south after we hit them." He traced his finger along the route. "Which means they'll send the search in the wrong direction." Hardin glanced up. "Any disagreements?"

There were none, and the meeting broke apart even faster than it assembled. Hardin didn't have to give any orders. Once everyone else had cleared the room, he turned to Tomas. "We've got a horse you can borrow."

"Obliged. Y'all move quick."

"One of the advantages of being small. Besides, we've been doing this for a bit. Enough that it's almost routine."

"They all military?"

Hardin shook his head. "Few, actually. But there's a lot of ways to learn the sword today, and the discipline is easy to teach when they all want to be part of what's happening."

In less than an hour they were all mounted and riding away from Alliston. Tomas didn't think he'd ever seen a raid come together so fast. He and Hardin rode beside each other near the front of the small column. Tomas glanced back at Alliston as they rode away. "You ever worry about what will happen when you're gone?"

"A little," Hardin confessed, "but I imagine it's no different than being a parent watching a child grow up and leave the house. I can't be around all the time, and I'm doing all I can to make sure the town doesn't need me."

After that, there was little conversation. They pushed the horses hard, leaving the forested area and the lakes for open prairie. Tomas wasn't too familiar with this part of the country, but he'd memorized the rough layout of the land when Hardin had unrolled his maps. They rode south and west, in the rough direction of the road where they hoped to intercept the caravan. Day soon passed into night, and they caught a few hours of sleep before mounting up again.

Tomas was grateful for the break. He hadn't expected the situation to evolve so quickly, and the brief rest did him good.

They rode throughout the next day and into the next night. It was the hardest riding Tomas had done in years, and his body let him know it. The healing he'd experienced at the nexus felt like it had happened years ago instead of the day before.

As they neared the road, they shifted direction. Hardin led them several miles farther west than they needed. They crossed the road, covering their tracks as well as they were able. Then they rode in a wide circle, approaching the ambush point from the south instead of the north.

Tomas understood Hardin's intent. Back in Alliston he'd claimed he was being cautious, and he was proving it here. The last thing they wanted was to be tracked back home.

It was smart, Tomas figured, but he wasn't sure it would be enough. Only a fool underestimated the church. They'd figure it out before long, especially if Hardin was a consistent nuisance in the area.

Finally, Hardin ordered them to set up camp. The riders dismounted and went about setting up camp with the same efficiency Tomas had come to expect from anything Hardin's people did. It wasn't more than ten minutes before food was ready and sleeping rolls were on the ground.

The group ate quietly and retired. Exhausted as Tomas was, he knew he wouldn't be able to sleep for a bit. He'd never been able to think well when he was mounted, and he needed some time. He wandered away to look at the stars without bothering any of the sleepers.

A few minutes later, he heard footsteps behind him. He turned, expecting Hardin. Instead, it was Myra. "Mind if I join you?" she asked.

"Please."

"Trouble sleeping?"

Tomas shook his head. "Not exactly. I'm tired enough, but y'all have given me a lot to think about."

"How's that?"

"Your settlements are the first places I've been in almost

half a year where I wouldn't die for revealing who I was. Recognize that for most people that isn't so much, but for me, it's a kindness I'm not sure I can repay. Likewise, I'm impressed by the way y'all work together. Haven't seen this kind of coordination since I was in the army, and even then it was only with a few units. You've got something special here."

"But?"

"But you might have heard that the things I get involved in don't end well. It worries me, is all."

Myra snorted. "Sure, but I'm not sure how that's your problem."

"Come again?"

"It's not your problem."

Tomas frowned. "Sorry, I'm not sure I follow. I don't want to bring trouble down on Alliston if I can help it."

"And I appreciate that, but it's not up to you. You're like some of my students, thinking that a flourish or extra feints are the keys to victory. I keep trying to tell them that nine times out of ten, simple is better. So let's make this simple: Do you want to join up with us?"

"Not quite certain, but yes."

"And Hardin wants you. So once you make up your mind, the matter is closed."

"But—"

Myra cut him off. "There are no buts. We're all adults here, and Hardin carries the weight of the town on his shoulders. If he wasn't sure, he'd ask for our thoughts and we'd figure it out together. We've already made our choice, and we're more than willing to see it through."

Tomas accepted the chastisement. "Sorry. Didn't mean to disparage you any. Just recently learned I need to think through my actions a bit more than I have in the past."

"No harm done. Thought something of the sort might be on your mind, and I'm glad I could make our position clear." She changed the subject so quickly it almost caused Tomas to stumble. "You got a favorite constellation up there? Mine's the hunter."

"The sleeper, actually."

Myra snorted. "Truly?"

"I know they're just stars, burning hundreds and thousands of light-years away, but I like thinking of the constellations as though they were real. And so I imagine a sleeper up there, looking down on all the chaos below and being able to relax despite all the noise we're making."

Myra shook her head. "Can't say I agree, but I suppose whatever brings you satisfaction is worth it." She yawned. "I think I'm going to turn in."

Tomas looked up at the stars. They always made him feel better, and Myra had helped, too. "I think I will, too. It's a big day tomorrow."

"Agreed. Any day we can punch the church in the nose is a good one."

8

———

They rose with the sun in the morning. Tomas sat up and stretched, then ran through the same forms he did most mornings. He found that for once, he wasn't alone in his morning practice. Both Emerson, a young swordsman covered head to toe in scars, and Myra did the same. It reminded Tomas of his younger days, working through the forms with his classmates.

Most of Hardin's squad watched him out of the corners of their eyes, but there was little for them to see. His daily forms were the same ones the sword schools had taught him as a child, the same forms that had propagated across the country. If they sought the secrets of Tomas' skill, they wouldn't find it in his morning practice.

Of course, he didn't think they'd find it anywhere. Tomas suspected Hardin was the better sword, and Myra was by far a better instructor. If Hardin's warriors sought more strength, the place to turn was to their own leaders.

After training, they broke their fast together, eating in relative silence. Once they finished their meals, Hardin ran one last time through their plan of attack, though there was little in the way of strategy to explain. They planned to hit the caravan where the road passed a rise in the land. They would hide on the other side of the rise, then hit the caravan hard. If the guards resisted, they sealed their fates. Otherwise, Hardin ordered his soldiers to avoid killing if they could.

That last bit surprised him, but it appeared he was the only one. None of the others made any comment, which made Tomas believe that letting guards live was a common practice. He tallied that as a reason why fighting with Hardin might work well for him.

One question bothered Tomas, because no one had asked it and it seemed an obvious one. "What if they have rifles?"

Hardin looked up from the map he'd spread before them. "Well, for one, I'd recommend not riding in a straight line." There were chuckles around the group, and Tomas wondered what he was missing. It didn't matter if they were hosts or not, a bullet was still plenty deadly. And even though they'd use the terrain as well as they could, they were still in rolling prairie. The caravan would have plenty of time to see them coming.

Hardin glanced over at one of his squad, a tall man with thin, corded limbs. "If they do, Kyle will take care of them."

Tomas had wondered about the man. Kyle was unique among the crew in that he only carried a short sword for steel. But he rode with a bow that seemed too large to be usable. The others seemed confident enough putting their lives in his hands, though, so Tomas figured that was good enough for him.

They broke camp and mounted their horses, riding hard for the ambush point. If Hardin's information was good, the squad expected the caravan to pass the ambush point sometime before mid-day. They reached the ambush well before then so they could be prepared.

Most of the group hid behind the rise while Myra crawled higher to watch the road. The others dismounted and waited. Some worked through their nerves by practicing their forms. Three got together and pulled out a pack of cards, resuming what looked to be a very long-running game.

Hardin approached. "You're welcome to stay back here if you want. You go to where Myra is, and you should be able to watch the whole party with a looking glass. It'll keep you out of sight, at least."

Tomas looked up at where the instructor lay, nearly invisible in the grass. "If you don't mind, I might just follow right behind you. I'll keep enough distance not to interfere with your coordination, but I'll stay close enough to help if something goes wrong."

Hardin fixed him with a questioning look. "You've made your decision, then?"

"I think I have."

Hardin clapped him on the back, a blow that landed almost hard enough to knock Tomas forward. "I'm glad to hear it! It's an honor to have you with us."

With that, Hardin moved on to the game of cards to speak with them. Tomas watched the man's back, slightly amazed. Acceptance was a simple thing, but after a long winter of being hunted wherever he turned, the giant man's welcome almost brought a tear to Tomas' eye.

Tomas turned his attention to Elzeth. "Ready for this?"

"So long as there aren't any rifles, this should be easy enough."

Tomas agreed. "Different, not to be fighting knights, isn't it?"

"I've long believed our lives would be much easier if you stopped picking fights with the strongest warriors wherever we went."

Tomas grunted. "Starting to think I might agree with you there."

It was midmorning when Myra crawled down from the summit of the rise. "They're here, right on time."

A wide grin lit Hardin's face, and Tomas saw another side to the man. Hardin wasn't a reluctant avenger. He was spoiling for a fight. Founding Alliston might very well be his legacy, but this, this was what he lived for. "If there's one thing you can count on the church for, it's being on time," he said. "Let's go."

Hardin's timing, much like everything else Tomas had observed, was nearly flawless. With Myra in the lead, they emerged from behind the rise no more than a quarter mile behind the caravan. Although it was only a small advantage, appearing from behind kept them out of sight of the caravan drivers and their escorts for a few precious seconds.

But the rumble of charging horses couldn't go unnoticed for long, and by the time Tomas had his horse up to a full gallop, the church guards had already spotted the group and were turning to engage.

Tomas took in the entire scene in a heartbeat. There were two wagons in the small caravan, each proudly bearing the three wavy lines that symbolized the church. Both wagons were covered, their contents hidden under thick canvas. Each wagon had two guards sitting up front. One drove while the other served as a lookout. Beyond that, there were four riders arranged in a loose formation around the caravan.

If all else were equal, Tomas would've assigned a small advantage to the defenders. The numbers of defenders and attackers were equal, and the lookouts had a more stable platform to fire bows or rifles from. But today, all things were not equal. These guards didn't know it yet, but they faced hosts. No matter how skillfully they fought, they had no chance.

As soon as the certainty crossed his mind, each of the guards riding lookout on the wagon drew a rifle from underneath the seat.

Tomas cursed and focused most of his attention on the barrels of those rifles. He prepared to turn his horse if either of the marksmen grew too interested in him.

The others seemed unconcerned, as if seeing two of the most dangerous weapons on the prairie appear was no more worrying than watching a cottontail rabbit approach their camp. Two horses ahead of him, Kyle casually nocked an arrow to his bow. Tomas watched, already impressed. Nocking an arrow while at full gallop was the sort of feat he only dreamed of being able to accomplish.

Kyle's skill didn't stop there, though. He drew the mighty bow back with what seemed to be no effort at all. Then he released the cord without hesitation.

Even with Elzeth burning Tomas had trouble tracking the arrow. It sped forward, punching into the rifleman's shoulder on the second wagon. The poor guard barely had a chance to raise his weapon. The impact knocked the marksman from his perch, and he fell from the wagon. He landed at an unnatural angle, but had the good fortune, if one could call it that, to miss the wheels of the wagon as it thundered past.

If he hadn't seen the shot with his own eyes, Tomas wasn't sure he would've believed it. The distance and the accuracy would have been impressive had both Kyle and the guard been standing still. But to hit such a shot at a gallop against the moving target?

No wonder Hardin and his group weren't concerned about the rifles.

The four riders still charged Hardin's band of thieves. For the moment, Tomas paid them little mind. The greatest danger was the rifleman on the lead wagon. What would he attempt after witnessing the other marksman's fate?

They found out soon enough, and Tomas couldn't fault the man's courage, though his wisdom was lacking. He brought the rifle to his shoulder and took aim at Kyle, but before he could pull the trigger one of Kyle's massive arrows caught him in the chest. The rifle went off, but the bullet shot harmlessly into the clouds. The rifleman collapsed back onto the seat of the lead wagon.

At the loss of their second rifle, Tomas expected the four riders to surrender. They had no cover left, and there couldn't be any doubt of Kyle's skill with the bow. Once might've been a fluke, but no reasonable person would charge Kyle after the performance he'd just given.

But these were believers, and they didn't fight like rational creatures. Tomas saw Kyle glance at Hardin, and Hardin gave him one sharp nod. Kyle loosed four more arrows in less than five seconds. Each one hit their target square. The closest rider had never gotten within fifty feet of Myra.

Now, certainly, the drivers had to surrender.

Again, as soon as Tomas had the thought, the caravan surprised him. Shadows emerged from under the canvas of the wagons, ready to fight.

Tomas swore. He would recognize those uniforms anywhere.

The wagons carried knights.

9

———

Tomas cursed even louder when one of the knights from the lead wagon pulled the rifle from the dead man's hands. Tomas kicked his horse and leaned forward in the saddle, hoping to reach the wagon before it was too late.

Ahead of him, Kyle noticed the knight's action and drew his bow back one more time. He launched his arrow, with all the power and precision of his previous shots. Tomas couldn't even follow the arrow. But the knight dropped low, pressing himself against the front bench with incredible speed. Kyle's arrow split nothing but the air above the knight's head.

The knight brought the rifle to bear, and Hardin, Tomas, and the others all pulled on the reins of their horses. What had been an organized charge turned into a chaotic mess as horses and riders sought some semblance of safety.

Tomas had only two goals. Don't get shot, and don't run into anyone else.

Not getting shot was by far the easier task. The eight of them had been riding too close together.

The front of the barrel flashed, and Tomas heard the

whine of a near miss as a bullet passed between him and Myra. A second shot followed less than a heartbeat later as the knight cycled the weapon. The second shot also passed wide, and Tomas allowed himself a quick sigh of relief. The knight fired quickly, but he couldn't aim.

Tomas didn't judge the knight too harshly. With a rifle in his own hands he would be little better. His weapon was and always would be a sword. And though they might disagree on almost all else, knights had the same opinion when it came to their preferred weapons.

What had been an easy battle turned into a nightmare. Each wagon had disgorged two knights, and on each wagon one knight had climbed up by the driver while the other guarded the back. Fortunately, the marksman on the second wagon had taken his rifle with him when Kyle's arrow had knocked him off his perch. But the wagons, which had once looked like tempting targets of opportunity, now looked like hardened fortresses. Kyle launched a few more arrows, but the knights were wary, and damned quick on their feet.

Tomas frowned as he watched them. These knights were good, even among their peers. Taking the wagons would be no easy task.

Tomas turned to Hardin. It would be his decision whether they continued or not. The way Tomas looked at it, there was no shame in turning tail and running. Hardin's first squad was impressive, but against four knights and a rifle, someone was going to die.

Hardin never so much as hesitated. He waved the group forward. Tomas held back for a moment, reconsidering the wisdom of their alliance. Had he been in Hardin's position, he would have made a different choice. The wagons weren't worth it.

But, Tomas supposed, if whatever was in those wagons

needed four knights guarding it, perhaps they were. There was something in those wagons the church desperately wanted kept safe.

In the end, he felt like he didn't have a choice. Not only had he given his word to support Hardin, he saw no future without Hardin's aid. He couldn't take on the church alone. He shouted and spurred his horse forward, angling for the lead wagon.

More shots rang out in quick succession, so close together it sounded almost like the rumble of thunder. Tomas did little besides hug himself close to his horse. The knight laid down an impressive amount of fire, but his aim remained poor. It probably didn't help that any time the knight tried to steady the barrel, Kyle launched an arrow his direction.

Tomas just pushed the horse forward as fast as he could, hoping none of the bullets found him. A minute later, Tomas had caught up to the back of the first wagon, his horse galloping about five paces behind. The knight on the back drew his sword, practically begging Tomas to get closer. Behind him, Myra was shouting something, but Tomas kept his attention ahead.

Only problem was, he had no idea how to get from his horse to the wagon without getting cut.

"Now what?" asked Elzeth.

Tomas stared at the wagon for a moment, then shook his head. Sometimes terrible ideas were the only way forward. "We've got to get on it."

"You can't be serious!"

"I need you, friend."

He gave Elzeth no time to argue. He pushed the horse harder, one last time. Five paces became four and then three. Time slowed down as Elzeth burned brightly. Tomas pulled his feet from the stirrups and climbed onto the back of the horse. Even with Elzeth's help, he wouldn't last long. He had a hard enough time riding a horse when he was properly seated. Balancing on top of one was nearly impossible.

Then the moment came. For one brief instant his feet felt stable underneath him.

He jumped.

The knight, of course, was waiting. But Tomas jumped higher than either of them expected, and the knight had to adjust the angle of his cut. Tomas drew his sword and thrust down, barely blocking the knight's attempt at cutting his legs off at the knees.

The contact between the blades twisted Tomas in the air, causing him to tumble roughly into the back of the second wagon. He hit the floor hard and almost lost his grip on his sword. He fought his way to his feet, then turned and rolled, twisting headfirst into a bench as the knight cut at him again. Tomas saw stars as he tried to focus on his enemy.

He might have made it onto the wagon, but he couldn't have put himself in a much worse position. The knight was balanced and ready, and his sword lashed out at Tomas constantly, its point flickering like a snake's tongue.

Damn, but the knight was fast. Elzeth burned brightly, but Tomas still suffered half a dozen cuts in the first exchange. And he still hadn't found his way to his feet.

There was a huge booming sound from somewhere far away, and Tomas feared the second wagon had yet another rifle. Unfortunately, there wasn't anything he could do about it. He had his own problems to deal with, and this knight didn't seem terribly interested in letting him live.

Then the knight's attention was pulled away for a moment by the sound of a second thump at the back of the wagon. Tomas and the knight both looked back to see Myra poke her head above the back of the wagon. "That's a lot harder than you made it look," she said.

Her head bobbed as she scrambled to get some sort of purchase with her feet and climb into the wagon.

The knight hesitated, torn between two targets that were as good as helpless before him. It was all Tomas needed to scramble to his feet. That focused the knight's attention on Tomas, and he struck out again, lightning quick.

But now Tomas was standing and Elzeth burned brightly within. Tomas avoided the blow and drove his shoulder into the knight's chest. The knight stumbled backward as Myra hauled herself higher and grabbed onto his tunic. She pulled hard, and the knight tumbled out the back of the wagon.

And somehow, against all odds, landed on his feet. Tomas stared, not believing what he saw. The knight chased after them, gaining on the wagon.

Myra was climbing and had no idea the danger she was in. Tomas took two quick steps and took position above her, guarding her with his sword. The knight eyed Tomas, then snarled and dropped back to the second wagon, which he hopped onto with ease.

Tomas swore at the sight, and Myra came to his rescue. Just as she had dismissed the knight she'd thrown off the wagon, he'd forgotten about the knight with the rifle. She shouted, and Tomas spun in time to see the knight jam the rifle barrel into the covered wagon, the end pointed right at Myra. At this distance, even the knight couldn't miss.

Tomas had time for one step, and he slapped the barrel away with the back of his blade, knocking it to the side just as it fired in front of his face.

The knight would've been better served by switching to

his sword. Though temporarily blinded and deafened, Tomas stabbed at where he knew the knight was, piercing the man's heart. The knight fell off the wagon, and Tomas enjoyed the distinct satisfaction of knowing that there was now one less knight that would plague the hosts.

Unfortunately, there were three left, and they didn't seem all that pleased that their first wagon had been robbed from underneath them. Tomas glanced back and saw the other wagon was gaining on them, and the two knights squished on the front bench with the driver looked angry enough to kill.

10

———

Tomas craned his neck to look for Hardin and the others. When he didn't immediately see them, he feared the worst, though he had no idea how it would have come to pass. Then he spotted horses, far behind the second wagon.

Why were they so far back?

Tomas couldn't guess the reason, but they weren't making any move to approach. He turned to Myra. "Looks like we're on our own."

He expected an objection. Or that she would have to look for herself. Instead, she nodded. "What next, then? Convince this driver to slow down?"

Instinctively, stopping the wagon felt like a mistake. In motion, they were a more difficult target. The other option was to have Myra drive the wagon, but Tomas suspected he would need her sword before long.

The choice was taken out of his hands before he could decide. The two knights, squished on the driver's bench, gestured toward the first wagon. After a brief discussion, they stood. The second wagon drew closer to the first, the horses only a few feet now from where Tomas waited. He frowned, realization dawning slowly.

As one, the knights leaped from the bench.

It was a suicidal jump. One that Tomas would consider only with Elzeth burning bright within him, and even then maybe only after a drink or three.

The knights were mirror images of one another. They each landed with one foot on a horse's back, then used that foot to leap toward the first wagon.

Tomas watched, mouth hanging open, as they made the impossible look simple. Too late, he realized the danger he was in. He snapped his sword up, but one of the knight's boots connected with his chin before he could do any good with it.

The kick snapped his head around, and the rest of his body followed. He spun and fell, sprawling across one of the benches that ran along the side of the wagon. Bright pinpoints of light danced in his vision, and even with Elzeth's help, they were slow to clear.

Myra, a step behind Tomas in the wagon, had another second to react, and that gave her enough time to get her sword up. The second knight, a thin man with long blond hair, cut at her, but Myra easily stepped away.

Tomas pushed himself to his feet, then almost tripped over a small crate. He took a step back to give himself some time. He was sure there were worse places to fight, but none came immediately to mind. The wagon rocked and rumbled over the rough path. Shadow and light warred in Tomas' vision as the sun fought to illuminate the interior of the wagon. And crates had been stacked haphazardly within. If Tomas had any advantage, it was that the knights were fighting against all the same elements.

Tomas stepped forward and cut, but the knight blocked.

Tomas wanted to move, but there was nowhere to go. The only space in the wagon was to his left, and if he stepped that direction he'd be cut down by Myra and her opponent. Tomas stabbed, but the knight swatted his sword aside.

Tomas preferred having space to move, to slice and cut at will. But again, the knight faced the same cramped space.

Survival wasn't always about who was strongest. It was about adaptation.

Tomas blocked a combination of awkward cuts from the knight. The knight paused, just to take a breath, and Tomas advanced. He stepped on one of the knee-high crates between him and the knight and launched an assault on the knight's head.

All he won for his efforts was a scratch above the knight's left ear.

Tomas advanced another pace, stepping off the crate and right next to the knight, who had no space to retreat. The knight cut at Tomas, but Tomas blocked it, and they locked swords as they snarled at one another.

The wagon suddenly tilted, as though the driver had run over a dead body. Both Tomas and the knight lost their balance, but the knight recovered faster. He planted his feet and shoved, and on only one foot, Tomas had no chance. He stumbled, then backpedaled before the back of his calves struck the same bench he'd been sprawled upon just a few moments before.

That sealed Tomas' fate. He pitched backward.

His head hit the canvas of the wagon and twisted at an unnatural angle. Then the wagon shifted again, and their locked swords sliced through the covering. The canvas tore, and after a few more seconds of struggle, Tomas found himself dangling nearly halfway out of the wagon.

Though closing the distance had been Tomas' idea, the knight had seized on it as his own. He was on top of Tomas, pushing down. He pressed his right hand against the backside of his blade, putting all his weight behind his considerable strength.

Tomas tried to throw the knight to either the left or the right, but the knight was having none of it. He shifted his weight with ease, balancing firmly on top of Tomas. The knight's sword inched closer to Tomas, cutting into his shoulders as the wagon jostled around. Elzeth burned bright, but it wasn't enough. The knight grinned triumphantly.

Tomas kicked his legs up. On flat ground, it would have been meaningless, but Tomas was balanced on the edge of the wagon. The kick tipped his weight over the side, and it was the one move the knight hadn't been expecting. They fell over together, and they both hit the ground hard.

The only difference was that Tomas had been ready. He landed on his shoulder and rolled, protected by Elzeth's strength. He came to a stop and cut at the knight before the surprised warrior even came to his feet. The cut sliced open the artery on the knight's neck. It was probably a fatal blow, but to make sure the host wouldn't heal, Tomas stabbed into the knight's heart.

The moment after the knight died, the second wagon rumbled by, and Tomas understood why the other members of Hardin's crew had fallen so far back. In the second wagon, a lone knight stood, but he stood with a stick of dynamite in one hand and a candle in the other. Their eyes met, and then the knight took in his dead comrade at Tomas' feet.

Tomas swore and sprinted after the second wagon. The knight lit the fuse on the stick of dynamite and held it in his hand as the fuse burned down. Tomas was gaining on the wagon, but it wouldn't be fast enough. The knight tossed the stick of dynamite at Tomas' feet, only a small fraction of the fuse left.

There was nowhere to run, and not even Tomas was good enough to cut the small fuse from the stick. On instinct alone, he swiped at the stick with the flat of his sword. It went flying into the air, exploding with enough force to cause Tomas to stumble.

He found his balance quickly and resumed the chase.

The knight was already casually lighting another stick. Elzeth burned just a bit brighter, and Tomas leaped for the wagon. He barely found his balance on the edge, but he managed to cut at the knight. The knight leaped back, and Tomas stepped deeper into the wagon.

The knight looked down at the lit stick of dynamite in his hands and his eyes went wide.

Unfortunately, the knight had made a mistake. The same one the rifle-bearing knight from the first wagon had. He'd chosen the wrong weapon. Now all he had in hand was a stick of dynamite and nowhere to throw it. Nor did he have a sword in hand to protect himself.

Tomas killed the knight, then sprinted forward. He clambered onto the driver's bench and kicked the driver off. Then he took a deep breath. If the knights could do it, he could, too. He leaped onto the horses, then across to the first wagon. Behind him, the second wagon exploded, wood and canvas flying in all directions.

Myra had triumphed over her knight, his body lying still on the wagon floor. She watched parts of the second wagon as they fluttered down to the ground. The victory hadn't come easy. She was bleeding from several cuts, although none of them looked immediately fatal. She glanced over at him, an appraising look in her eyes.

"You really do make a mess of things when you get involved, don't you?" she asked.

11

———

Myra and Tomas stopped their wagon with little difficulty. Though the driver was a believer, even he recognized there was nothing he could do. Rather than die needlessly, he slowed the wagon to a stop. Myra escorted him from the wagon and tied his hands behind his back and his ankles together.

Hardin handed out his orders, and the group split into teams. Myra and Emerson mounted their horses to track down the second driver and bring him back. Kyle led a group to the site where the second wagon had exploded to search for anything useful. Hardin and Tomas searched the first wagon while keeping an eye on the secured driver.

They elected to pull the church supplies from the wagons and into the light of day. There were nearly a dozen crates of varied sizes, but with the two of them working together, the task was soon completed.

"Impressive display back there," Hardin said.

"Just trying to help."

Hardin grunted. "You always fight like that?"

"More often than I'd care to admit."

His answer was greeted with several seconds of silence. Then, "Thanks. You might be a damned fool, but you saved some of my squad's lives today. I won't forget that."

"Any time."

Once they finished moving the crates out of the wagon, Hardin attacked them with a crowbar, starting with the largest ones first. Nails screeched in protest as Hardin pried them out, and one by one the crates were opened.

Given the presence of the knights, Tomas suspected gold or weapons. Or parts to some sort of new weapon that would justify the rumors he'd been hearing. Instead, the first several crates were filled with worked metal packed in straw. Tomas examined each piece, trying to figure out what was so valuable about the metal. As near as he could tell, the answer was "nothing."

The metalwork had been hammered out by master craftsmen. Most of it was thin, no thicker than a few sheets of paper. Some of the pieces looked like they connected with bolts, but Tomas couldn't make heads or tails of the grand design.

Tomas held up one of the pieces and showed it to the driver. "Don't suppose you have any idea what this is?"

All he received in response was an angry glare.

They broke into another crate, only to find more of the same.

Myra and Emerson returned first, with the other bound driver tossed over the back of Myra's horse. They deposited the driver a few feet from the other, then came to inspect the loot. "Anything exciting?" Emerson asked.

Hardin held up one of the pieces of metal. "Only this, so far."

The next crate was a size smaller, but when Hardin pried it open all they found was a long spool of copper wire.

The others arrived soon after, carrying bent and twisted pieces of metalwork similar to those Hardin and Tomas had been finding. They tossed some of the larger pieces at Hardin's feet.

Myra gave voice to what they were all thinking. "Given the knights, I was expecting something more exciting. Why would they waste knights on *this*?"

"Maybe this wasn't the most important part of the delivery," Tomas said.

Every eye turned to him.

"At least two of those knights were hosts," Tomas explained.

"Come again?" Hardin said.

Myra came to Tomas' rescue. "I agree. The knight I fought was too fast to be only human."

There was a disdain in her voice when she said "only human" that sent a shiver up Tomas' spine, but he didn't have time to worry. Hardin had turned to him. "You think maybe the host knights were the delivery?"

"Most unusual thing we've come across so far today."

Tomas swore to himself. Why was it that with the church there were always more questions than answers? The church hated the sagani and their human allies, and the knights were trained specifically to kill hosts. The last time Tomas had come across a knight hosting a sagani, the man had been mad. Not from the sagani, but from going against everything he had ever believed.

Were they trying to create more assassins like Ghosthands?

That was a truly terrifying thought.

But it also didn't sit quite right with him. Ghosthands had been something different. Despite being hosts, the knights had still fought like knights. Unless they were traveling to Kimson to train to become more like Ghosthands?

Tomas shook his head. He could speculate for days on what the church intended. Hells, he'd spent no small part of the winter doing just that, and he wasn't any closer, yet, to the truth.

Hardin grunted. "Well, suppose we should take a look at what's left," he said. He gripped his crowbar tightly and went to work on the other crates. Kyle pulled a crowbar from his saddlebags and helped.

They discovered more of the same. As the crates got smaller, the metalwork within got more delicate, but none of them could make sense of what they were seeing. The disappointment was clear on everyone's faces.

Tomas didn't feel the same. Sure, it wasn't gold or weapons, or anything else that was immediately valuable, but the church had gone to a lot of trouble to keep this shipment safe. And now it was theirs. One way or another, they'd hurt the church today. Even though it raised new questions, those questions meant Tomas was getting closer to the answers.

The last crate was the smallest, but Tomas remembered that it had been heavy. Kyle and Hardin attacked it together. But as soon as the lid came off, disaster struck.

Tomas wasn't watching the moment it happened, but he turned when he heard Hardin curse. He spun around, just in time to see Kyle dive straight at the crate, arm outstretched.

Hardin reacted with incredible speed. He caught Kyle's wrist and pulled it away from the crate. Kyle snarled and lashed out, but Hardin was retreating, pulling both of them away from the recently opened container. Kyle strained against Hardin, then succeeded in tossing the giant man out of the way.

Tomas recognized the signs of madness, but the sudden shift caught him as flat-footed as the others. His eyes flicked down to the open crate, and the realization struck like a thunderclap. A very familiar blue glow emanated from within.

Elzeth flared to life, burning bright once more. Tomas and Kyle both ran for the crate, but Tomas was just a bit closer to start. He leaped across the top of the crate and tackled Kyle, whose attention was fully on the crate. The two of them went down in a tangle of limbs.

Everything happened at once.

Tomas' tackle shook everyone out of their surprise, and they all rushed forward. Kyle kicked at Tomas, landing several painful blows as Tomas focused more on keeping Kyle away from the crate than protecting himself. Out of the corner of his eye, he saw the two drivers start to struggle with their bonds as everyone's attention was elsewhere.

"STAY AWAY!" Hardin's voice thundered across the prairie, so commanding even Tomas almost obeyed. The others stopped in place, and even the drivers froze. Tomas still wrestled with Kyle, but then Hardin joined the fight.

Tomas wrapped up one of Kyle's arms, surprised by the thin man's wiry strength. He was hot, too. His sagani had to be burning bright.

Elzeth responded in kind, and together, Hardin and Tomas finally succeeded in pulling Kyle away from the crate. The farther away they got, the less pronounced Kyle's struggles became. Eventually, he went limp in their arms. Hardin waved for the others, who hurried over.

"Everybody stays away from that crate," Hardin ordered. "Kyle's going to be fine, I think. But that's a dangerous crate for us to handle." He turned to Tomas. "Mind checking it out? I don't want to get too close, myself."

Tomas agreed. He left the others and crouched down next to the crate. The first thing he noticed was that the crate had been lined in metal. It was no wonder the thing had been so heavy. The blue glow emanated from underneath straw packing. He grabbed his knife and brushed the straw out of the way. Even though he knew what he was going to find, he was still surprised when the gems were revealed. "You ever seen any that size before?" he asked Elzeth.

"Not that I remember."

Inside the crate wasn't one stone, but more than a dozen tiny gems. Even Tomas felt a tremendous pull as he uncovered them. He resisted the urge to touch them, but he did lean forward for a closer look. They were as large as a diamond for a ring, and each had been cut by a gem smith. Tomas licked his lips.

Now he understood at least part of why the knights had been guarding this caravan.

Tomas stood back up. He returned to Hardin, who was speaking with the others.

"It's not just one nexus in there, but over a dozen. All of them tiny enough to be jewelry."

Hardin glanced down at Kyle. "It's no wonder, then. I can even feel the pull here."

"How close is Kyle, to the end?" Tomas asked.

Hardin shrugged. "Hard to say. He doesn't have many tics, but something is happening inside his mind. He doesn't talk much anymore, and sometimes it seems as though he's a child again. Probably not more than a few months, if I had to guess."

"Might be that because his sagani is stronger he didn't

have a chance once that crate was opened."

Hardin frowned. "Could be." He pointed at the crate. "You ever see anything like that before?"

"No. I know the church has been obsessed with the nexuses for a while now, but it never occurred to me they might be altering them." Tomas looked over at the drivers, who were now watching the unfolding scene with undisguised interest. "Let me try something."

Tomas searched driver's bench of the first wagon and found a pair of leather gloves. He put them on and stared down at the crate. "Ready in case this doesn't work?"

"As I'll ever be," Elzeth said.

Tomas reached down and picked one of the stones up. It glowed in his hand, but the leather protected him from the usual effects of the nexus. Tomas made a fist around the stone, then walked over toward the drivers. They watched him with wary looks, but there was nowhere for them to run. Tomas let the stone drop until it was between his thumb and forefinger. Then he pressed it against the forehead of one of the drivers.

Nothing happened.

"What are you doing?" the driver asked. He tried to struggle away, but Tomas kept the stone pressed firmly against his forehead. Still, nothing happened.

Tomas pulled the stone away and palmed it. "You have any idea what these are for?"

The driver shook his head. "They don't tell me any more than I need to know. My only task was to get them to the mission at Kimson."

"You were to give them to the priest there?"

"Was supposed to turn over everything there."

"Do you know if anything was to come back?"

"Didn't know for sure, but I'd doubt it. Most trips we're

only carrying things one way. Not much going back east right now."

Tomas saw no reason to doubt the driver's sincerity. The church was a secretive organization, and it didn't surprise Tomas that the driver knew little.

Tomas returned to Hardin.

He'd learned something else important, too. The stones didn't affect normal humans. The driver hadn't so much as blinked. Tomas had long been fairly certain the nexuses and the sagani were somehow connected. This, more than any other evidence, proved it.

"Driver doesn't know much," Tomas said.

Hardin thought for a moment, then approached the pair of drivers. He squatted down in front of them. "You two been to Kimson before?"

The drivers looked to one another, as though daring the other to speak first. Eventually, the one on Tomas' left answered Hardin with a question. "What if we have? What's it to you?"

"I'm a curious man," Hardin answered. When he saw the explanation wasn't good enough for them, he shrugged. "Life's getting hard out here for bandits. Wondering if maybe there's some riches in Kimson that might make it worth our time to plan a visit."

The driver on the right let out one short, mocking laugh. "Please do. Town ain't much more than the mission, some homes, and a few businesses. But it's got enough fighters there to make the likes of you piss your pants and run the other way."

The first driver hissed at the second. "These aren't just skilled bandits, Clay."

Hardin stood. "True enough."

He drew his sword and cut the drivers down.

12

————

Tomas stepped forward, his hand instinctively reaching for the hilt of his sword.

Right away, he knew it was the wrong move. His allies turned on him, reacting to the hint of aggression with all the protectiveness a mother bear had for her cubs. Each and every member of Hardin's first squad tensed and took combat stances. No steel was drawn, but all they needed was the slightest excuse. Hardin snapped the blood from his blade and held out his left hand to calm the crowd. "Easy now, we're all friends here. No need for any of this."

"You didn't have to kill them," Tomas said.

Hardin's expression was as cold as ice on a cloudy winter day. "And what would you have done?" He gestured toward the bodies. "They both saw your face. Talked with you. They both knew that you held the shards of a nexus in your hands, even if they didn't know their importance. Just how do you think this was going to end?"

Hardin delivered each line with a quiet certainty, and from the expressions on the faces of the others, Tomas knew he would find no support among Hardin's followers. They accepted his worldview with all the eagerness that believers accepted the teachings of the church. Tomas clenched his fists but let his arms relax by his side, away from his sword.

Of course, he understood Hardin's argument. Even if they had somehow extracted a promise of silence from the drivers, they were dealing with believers. The minute they were questioned by any member of the church, the truth of the matter would come out. And the church's reaction would be just as predictable. However intense the manhunt for Tomas had been over the brutal winter, it would be nothing compared to the pursuit that would result if the church knew he was the one who had stolen the shards. They would send every knight and every soldier they could spare after him.

But that wasn't even the worst of it. Scarier than all of that, Ghosthands would know where Tomas had been. As wide and expansive as the frontier was, it wouldn't be big enough. They wouldn't leave any stone unturned in their hunt for him.

Had he been alone, the story might have been different, the risk bearable. But it wasn't just his life at stake here. The drivers had seen Kyle's out-of-control behavior, and the one driver had guessed they were dealing with hosts. It wouldn't take long for someone to understand that Tomas had finally found some allies in his war. And once that truth was discovered, the inevitable outcome was without question. All of Ulva's greatest fears about Hardin would come to pass.

Tomas knew all of this, but the sight of the dead captives still twisted his stomach. But he nodded and took a step back.

Hardin sheathed his blade, which caused the others to stand up straighter and relax. The tension wasn't gone, but it faded to a point where Tomas wasn't worried he'd have to fight again today. Without turning from Tomas, Hardin ordered the others to gather up everything that was valuable and pack their horses for the escape.

The squad dispersed, leaving Hardin and Tomas alone. Hardin stepped closer so that he could speak quietly. "Is this going to be a problem?"

Tomas surrendered this battlefield. "You're right enough. Can't deny that. Doesn't mean it doesn't feel wrong, though."

Hardin fixed him with a hard stare. "If you're serious about joining us, that sense of mercy might get you in trouble. This is the church were fighting against, and you know damn well they won't show an ounce of compassion for us if our roles were reversed."

"I think the wanted posters flying around all over the country can tell you well enough that I'm not afraid to get my hands bloody. But don't think for a moment that means I'll just kill anyone with the crest. It's not how we win this war. I learned that well enough at Chesterton."

Hardin spit at Tomas' feet. "Just remember. It's not just about you anymore. You get discovered while you're with us, and that's a hell of a lot of innocent people you're putting at risk. Think on that."

The two glared at each other for a moment more, and then Tomas nodded. They understood one another well enough.

Hardin looked toward the crate. "You mind holding the shards for us? Truth be told, I'm nervous to have my own too close to those things. You seem more resistant than the rest of us."

Tomas had been thinking the same. "Sure thing. I might hang back a little on the ride, especially as Kyle's reaction was so strong."

Hardin gave a sharp nod. "Good." He paused. "Thanks, again."

"Happy to help."

Hardin grunted, then went to supervise the thievery. Tomas looked one last time at the bodies of the two drivers, then went to collect the shards.

They sorted through the spoils quickly, displaying the same practiced efficiency with looting that Tomas was starting to take as the hallmark of all their efforts. The hosts operated with a fair degree of independence, and they seemed to share a sense of what was valuable and what wasn't. Tomas was surprised to see them load their saddlebags with much of the worked steel.

When they rode away, every person's saddlebags were filled to bursting. They'd even loaded Tomas down with steel he had no interest in.

Curious, Tomas asked Hardin why they bothered. Steel was plentiful and cheap, even on the frontier. Hardin's reply was decisive. "It may not be the most expensive thing we've ever stolen, but I figure that if they want it, taking it from them hurts. Besides, you've seen the quality of that work. Might not have cost much in gold, but they invested a lot of time in it."

While they loaded saddlebags, Tomas secured the crate with the shards of the nexus. On a whim, he put the lid of the crate back on top.

"You feel anything?" Tomas asked Elzeth.

"It's still there, but faint."

Tomas lifted the lid and the pull returned. Something about the metal must have been dampening the pull of the nexus. It made his choice easy. Tomas straightened the nails and hammered them back in as well as he could before securing the crate to his horse.

Just to be safe, Tomas encouraged the others to pull ahead of him. No sense risking another host sliding into madness, and besides, he needed some time to himself. They kept an easier pace running away from the scene than they did riding to it. The caravan wasn't due to arrive in Kimson for another couple of days, and it would probably be another day on top of that before the settlement's concern justified putting together a search party. Any meaningful pursuit was at least a week away, and by then they would be well gone.

Ahead of him, the others talked among themselves as they rode. Tomas couldn't help but feel a tinge of envy. It had been too long since he'd run with a crew, and he found he longed for the company.

After a minute, he shook his head and grunted in disdain. The winter must have been harder on him than he thought.

Elzeth tried to slumber, but Tomas felt the sagani's restlessness. Though Tomas didn't feel the pull, Elzeth was more sensitive to the nexuses. Elzeth's typical post-battle rest eluded him.

He felt bad disturbing Elzeth, but the sagani wasn't sleeping. "When we get back, I think we're going to need to spend more time with these stones. Maybe Hardin's nexus, too."

Elzeth grumbled at the thought. "You know touching those stones is the most dangerous thing we do, right? And that's saying something, considering your lifestyle."

"Dunno. Might put dueling Ghosthands at the top of that particular list."

"And you'll notice we've spent half a year running from him."

Tomas acknowledged the point. "Still, don't see a better way of learning the truth. I'd be happy if there was."

Elzeth didn't argue further, but Tomas sensed the matter was far from settled.

The next several days passed in a blur. Hardin and the others went to no small trouble to disguise their tracks. They rode through streams, doubled back on their own trail, and split up into different groups, rendezvousing only after they'd put miles behind them. They spent more than a full day traveling farther south before they turned toward home.

Tomas wasn't sure that all their efforts made them impossible to track, but they were about as close as humanly possible. If Tomas had harbored any doubts about Hardin's desire to keep Ulva and the others safe, they were banished for good now.

But because of those efforts, Tomas spent longer in the saddle than he had in ages, and his legs cried in relief when Jonasson came into view. He swore that he wouldn't ride a horse again for a month, if not longer.

But it wasn't his legs that caught most of his attention when he saw the town. It was the feeling in his chest. He felt his body relax as the sounds of hammers and saws washed over him. The feeling was one he hadn't had in a damned long time. So long, it took him a while to understand it.

When he saw Jonasson, he felt like he was home.

13

───────

Tomas followed the rest of Hardin's first squad to the stables near the outskirts of Alliston, where he went through the routine of unsaddling his horse. The others, clearly more familiar both with their mounts and with the process, finished well before him. Thankfully, Myra came over and volunteered to finish the task for him. Tomas accepted gratefully, but before he could escape the stables he heard the sound of running feet.

They all looked to the stable doors to see Ross come skidding to a stop. Tomas almost laughed out loud. Every time he and Ross crossed paths, the young man was running one place or the next. Ross took a moment to catch his breath, then searched the stables with his gaze.

Tomas' stomach sank when Ross' eyes stopped on him. "Ulva wants to see you," he announced. Ross glanced over at Hardin. "Soon as you're able, that is."

Tomas could guess enough what Ulva wanted, and figured there was no point trying to avoid the argument. "Sure thing. I'll be there when I can."

Ross took that as his cue to leave. He gave Hardin a bow, then ran off to deliver Tomas' message to the mayor.

Tomas went over to where Hardin was helping sort the loot from the caravan. He carried the crate of shards, drawing every eye in the stable. Hardin looked like he wanted to flinch away from the box. "You want these?"

Hardin licked his lips as though he was being presented a perfectly seared steak. Then he shook his head. "Best you hold onto them for now, I think. Probably goes without saying, but don't spend too much time around a single host. I know with the lid on it's not bad, but I'm worried what happens if that lid gets open. There's several hosts around here like Kyle. Best to be careful."

Tomas agreed. He tucked the crate under his arm and went to go see Ulva. He wished, more than anything, the crate wasn't quite so heavy.

He left Alliston and crossed the empty land between it and Jonasson. As he passed a tree, he noticed a hole in the trunk almost perfectly sized for the crate. Hiding the shards here might be safer than bringing them into a town filled with hosts, but he couldn't bring himself to let them go. He continued on, entering the outskirts of town a few minutes later.

The first thing he noticed was that all traces of his anonymity were gone. It stood to reason, of course. Word always got out, and his presence was newsworthy, considering the risk it carried. The reactions he received were mixed. At best, people seemed cautiously neutral, but many glared at him as though he was a conquering villain. Tomas ignored both reactions as well as he was able, but made quick time to Ulva's house.

He also noticed the way people drifted towards him. The motion was subtle enough he suspected most didn't even realize what was happening. But the shards pulled at the hosts. He hurried a little faster, breathing a sigh of relief when Ulva's small home came into view. He found her just as he had before, sitting on the rocker and watching the town with a smile on her face.

The smile disappeared as soon as he approached. She glared down at him from her rocker. "Well, if you aren't a match for Hardin, I don't know who is. You were here less than a day before you went riding off to cause mischief."

The words were bitter, but Tomas caught the resignation in her voice. Tomas tilted his head in her direction. "Sorry to prove all your suspicions correct, ma'am. Something came up, and I would have felt a fool for passing up on the opportunity."

Ulva raised a skeptical eyebrow, fixing him with a stare that lasted long enough to make him uncomfortable.

Then she stood and gestured for him to follow her. He did, grateful for the relative privacy of her home. He put the crate down just inside her door. As before, she fussed with a hot kettle and soon had tea prepared for him.

Tomas was about to launch into an explanation of his behavior, but she cut him off. "I don't much care, and as I've said before, I'm not really in charge here. Just trying to do what's right for the people who call this place home." She took a deep breath. "I want you to leave, Tomas. What will it take for you to agree with me?"

Tomas leaned back. Her directness caught him by surprise, and it took him a moment to recover. "Hardin tells me you two have had many discussions over the years."

"We have." She waited for Tomas to get to his point.

He obliged. "I agree with what Hardin believes. As much as I respect your ideals, there's only so long these settlements will last if you're not willing to fight for them."

"But you're not fighting for us. You're fighting for yourself."

He liked that she didn't pull her punches. "True, but I believe our interests serve one another."

"And what happens when they don't?" Ulva suddenly waved her hand, cutting off the conversation. "Hells, you two are alike. Never mind that."

At his questioning glance, she explained. "The same thing happens when Hardin and I get together. We'll get pulled this way and that by some small detail that doesn't really matter." She set her teacup down. "You seem like a decent enough fellow, Tomas. You've got your beliefs and you stick by them. I can respect that. But you have to see that your being here puts everything these people are building at risk. I can't force you to leave, but these old bones aren't above begging. So will you do it? Will you leave?"

The question was asked with such hope and such sincerity that it caused Tomas to reconsider.

She saw that she had him uncertain, and she had the rare wisdom to fall silent and let him argue with himself.

Tomas bit his lower lip. She was right, and Hardin was right, and he couldn't choose between them. He should leave, but how could he, when he kept getting closer to answers?

He stood up and went over to the crate. He put on the leather gloves he had taken from the wagon, then pried the lid off. He watched her for an adverse reaction. To him, the pull felt even stronger than before. But she seemed fine. He reached in and pulled a stone out, then brought it over and displayed it to her. "Do you know what these are?"

Her expression told him all he needed to know. "Never seen one that small, or cut."

"But you've come across nexuses before."

"Aye, I have. Hardin's little secret isn't as much of a secret as he likes to think."

There was something in her voice, something he couldn't put his finger on, that gave her away. In a leap of intuition, Tomas knew. "You've touched one."

A sly smile spread across her face. "I have."

"You're the first person besides me that I know of who has ever touched one and lived to tell about it."

"Lucky me."

Elzeth chimed in. "Perhaps that's why her sagani feels so much different." He churned in Tomas' gut. "I wonder if I feel the same to other sagani?"

Tomas didn't have an answer to that, but Ulva's question was the more important one. How could he leave, though, knowing that someone else here had touched a nexus and lived to tell about it? "What do you know about these?" he asked.

She sensed his desire and wasn't above turning it against him. "A lot, and still not enough. What are the answers worth to you?"

Inspiration struck Tomas. "How about I make you a deal? A promise."

"I'm listening."

"More than anything, I need to understand what the church is doing. And it pains me to admit it, but I don't think I can do it alone. So help me. These stones were heading to Kimson. If you can help me figure out what they were intending these for, and let me work with Hardin to stop their plans, I'll leave as soon as it's over."

"How will you decide when it's over?"

"I won't." His hand closed around the shard and he returned it to the crate. "You will."

"You promise to honor your word?"

"I do, so long as you act in good faith."

Ulva sipped at her tea while she considered Tomas' offer. "Convince Hardin to stop his raids for a year after, then you have yourself a deal."

Tomas scoffed, remembering how Hardin had led them into battle. "Are you serious? I'd have better luck convincing a mountain lion to become a pet."

Ulva laughed. "True enough, but I think you might be the only person Hardin will listen to. So it's worth trying. And to sweeten the deal, I'll tell you this..." She leaned forward, keeping him in suspense.

"I know *a lot* about the nexuses. If you *can* convince him of our deal, I'll tell you everything I've learned over my years of study."

14

When Tomas stepped from Ulva's porch, he felt a sudden urge to sit down on her weathered rocking chair, kick back his feet, and relax for a spell. There was a brief moment, before anyone noticed he'd emerged, when he glimpsed the true nature of Jonasson.

Down the street two men were deep in conversation, smiles wide across their faces as they gestured toward an unfinished house. A woman passing by carried a load of fresh laundry from the lake, humming a catchy melody, her steps in rhythm with the tune in her head. Farther away, a pair of hammers sounded an even beat as yet another house was added to the growing town.

It was all so—normal—Tomas supposed. The scene could have been taken out of any town growing across the frontier. A visitor, wandering in with no prior knowledge of the town, would never guess they walked down streets filled with hosts.

It was a dream made true thanks to the will and effort of Ulva. Perhaps others might criticize its mundanity, but they would never understand. To be a host was to carry a hidden brand, to fear that at any moment it might be exposed to the light of public scrutiny. That fear didn't exist here, and that was something precious worth fighting for.

Then the others on the street noticed him, and his urge to kick back and relax fled. The two men stopped their conversation as the smiles fell from their faces. The woman with the laundry stopped humming and scurried down the street as though she'd seen a ghost.

Tomas tucked the crate under his arm again and pretended not to notice.

On his way out, though, one question troubled him more than he cared to admit. If he wasn't welcome here, where would he be?

As it turned out, the answer to his question was only a half-mile away. The short distance between the two settlements had never felt so empty, and the differences between the settlements had never seemed so stark.

If Jonasson was the epitome of frontier normalcy, Alliston was the opposite. Warriors hurried from task to task, driven by a sense of deadly purpose. Their response to him was as different from Ulva's town as could be. Word of his identity must have finally spread, because he received nothing but awe-inspired stares and deep bows of respect as he walked down the street.

None of it made him feel like he belonged. He was honored, certainly, but not at ease. They welcomed him, but not as one of them. He was more of a symbol than a man. He returned their bows but made haste to Hardin's house. The crate under his arm grew heavy as he feared what would happen if he came too close to a host near the end of their life. Hardin's front door couldn't come soon enough.

When Tomas knocked on the door, Hardin called out

through an open window. "Door's always open, Tomas. Just come on in."

Tomas did, depositing the crate next to the door. He followed the smell of cooking meat to the kitchen, where Hardin cooked over a wood-fired stove. The man barely glanced up. "Hungry?"

"Starving."

"Pull up a seat. Food will be ready soon."

Tomas grabbed one of the chairs from the dining room and pulled it to the kitchen door. Hardin talked while he cooked. "I imagine she wanted you to leave."

"Practically begged me to."

"And?"

"We made a deal."

Hardin barked a laugh. "Do tell."

Tomas did, concluding his summary with his agreement to get Hardin to cease his attacks on the church for a year. He finished his story right about the time Hardin finished cooking. The rebel leader transferred the steaks to plates, and they moved the conversation to the dining room.

"She's a force of nature," Hardin admitted. "Claims she hates being called the mayor, which is true enough, but none of this would exist without her." He cut into his steak and shoved an enormous bite in his mouth. "So, go ahead, I want to know how you thought you'd convince me."

Tomas took a bite himself before answering. He pointed his thumb over his shoulder, at the crate where the shards rested. "I don't think it will be all that hard. You know as well as I do that those change everything."

Hardin grunted as he bit into his meat. Tomas took it as a sign to continue.

"Don't know what your average raid looks like, or what kind of loot you're taking from the church, but I'm guessing it doesn't qualify as much more than a nuisance. You can't risk doing more. Not right now. But those—the loss of those will catch the church's attention. You were going to have to switch up your operations anyway. Only difference is I'm going to give you a way to make it all matter."

"How so?"

"By helping me. Instead of these risky raids that only annoy the church, I want you to help me hit Kimson. I want to figure out what the church uses nexuses for, and I want to destroy whatever they're working on. All I ask for is one raid, more dangerous than anything you've yet attempted. If it succeeds, maybe we actually put some hurt on them. And if it succeeds, you'll need to lie low for a while anyway. A year seems about right. It would give you enough time to really focus on preparing Alliston for the future."

Hardin leaned back in his chair. "When you're a host, or at least, a normal host," he said, nodding in Tomas' direction, "a year is no small amount of time. It might very well be most of what I have left."

"Which means you should make it count. This would matter more than anything else you could do."

"But then I'd be giving my word to stop for a year. I wouldn't be able to press my advantage."

Tomas shook his head, then swept his left hand across the room, indicating the whole settlement around them. "You're thinking about your efforts too narrowly."

"How so?"

"I think that what you build is far more important than what you fight against. No matter what you accomplish against the church, it will pale in comparison to what you and Ulva are creating here. This lets you focus on what you can build, what you can leave behind for the hosts that follow in our wake."

Hardin thought about it for a good while, and Tomas used the opportunity to finish his steak. Though the meal satisfied his hunger, it did little else. Hardin was an incredible sword, but he didn't belong anywhere near a kitchen.

Finally, Hardin nodded. "Fair enough. If this hits them as hard as you claim it will, I'm in."

15

Ulva might have been a host, but she didn't move like one. She moved like an old lady, picking her way gingerly around exposed tree roots and sharp stones. It was less than a mile from Alliston to Hardin's nexus, but at this rate, they'd spend over half the day just getting there.

"I still can't believe you convinced him," Ulva said.

"If all this hurts the church as much as we hope it will, he'd need to lie low anyway. This works well for him, too, though he's probably loath to admit it."

Ulva stopped before an exposed root, staring at it as though she was planning a complicated military advance instead of her next step.

"You sure you don't want me to pick you up?" Tomas asked.

Ulva cackled. "You may want to get your hands on me, young man, but I assure you that I'm not so easily caught."

Tomas barely managed not to roll his eyes. "I was thinking more that it might allow us to reach the nexus faster, and you'll have more energy once we arrive."

"Of course you were."

Tomas rubbed his eyes. He still couldn't tell when she was serious and when she was mocking him. He suspected it was far more often the latter. But she did start walking faster, so he let her comments slide. He changed the subject to what he was most curious about. "When did you first touch a nexus?"

"Not until I came here. It wasn't long after we started building. I was out one afternoon, surveying the area. As you might expect, the glowing blue stone caught my attention. Looking back on it, probably wasn't the smartest idea to reach out and touch it, but I had a powerful urge to do so."

"The sagani are drawn to them."

"True enough. Probably would have figured that out on my own back then if I'd had half a brain and thought about it for more than a second. But what's done is done. I touched it, as excited as though I'd found a vein of gold."

"What was it like for you?"

"Not pleasant. It welcomed the sagani within me, but it wanted nothing to do with me."

Tomas noted her phrasing, and it reminded him of something Narkissa had said as they'd walked toward Chesterton. "You haven't named your sagani?"

Ulva snorted. "I heard you named yours. Elroy, or something like that?"

Elzeth chuckled at that. Seeing as he took no offense, Tomas didn't either. "Elzeth."

"You talk to it, too?"

"Don't you?" Tomas was aware that plenty of hosts didn't talk to their sagani, but the only reason their contact with the nexus hadn't torn Elzeth away was because Elzeth didn't want to leave. Tomas assumed that the nature of their relationship was at least part of the reason why he could survive touching the stones no other host could. It stood to reason, then, that Ulva would have a similar relationship.

"I suppose I've shouted at it a few times, back when I had first become a host and was furious at it and the world. But to answer the spirit of your question, no, I don't talk to it."

"Why not?"

"Why would I?" Ulva looked at him, studying him as though she was seeing him for the first time. "What's it like for you?"

Tomas felt like he should be the one asking the questions, but there was something more to this misunderstanding, a deeper truth he'd been nibbling at the edges of for almost a year now. He considered how best to describe his experience as a host. "It's like having a close friend, or maybe a beloved family member, staying with you. Elzeth spends most of his time resting, but I also always know he's there, ready at a moment's notice. But when we talk, it's almost exactly like how you and I are talking now."

"Just...conversation? You don't feel its, sorry, Elzeth's, emotions?"

"No, I do. And he feels mine, but it's not like knowing exactly what the other person is thinking."

"So you'd consider yourself separate entities?"

"Most of the time. In dire straits, we'll unify."

Ulva nodded, as though he'd said something important. But for the life of him, he couldn't figure out what it might be.

"I've talked with a lot of hosts over the years. Maybe more than anyone else, probably." Ulva hopped lightly over an exposed root, and Tomas realized that her slow pace from earlier had been either a prank or a test. Old as she was, she moved like someone decades younger. "Maybe some successful inquisitors have talked with more, but I'd doubt it. You know what I've learned?"

Tomas was sorely tempted to cut at her with a snarky comment, but held his tongue. "No."

"Most hosts have been given a gift, a precious gift. But they're like greedy children on their birthdays, ripping open the present, barely glancing at what's inside, and going on to the next gift. No one spends any time exploring what they've received. I thought you might be different. I thought you might have figured it out, given how long you've been a host."

"You're saying I haven't?"

Ulva didn't answer his question, which was rapidly becoming a frustrating habit. "Whose idea was it, that Elzeth would rest most of the time?"

Tomas tried to remember. That conversation had happened many, many years ago. "His, I think. We'd been talking about ways to prolong our lifespan, and he believed that madness came quicker the more a host used their ability. It matched roughly with what I observed, and from that day forward, we made a pledge to use our ability as little as possible."

Ulva grunted. They were getting close to the nexus now, and Tomas still felt as though he didn't have any answers. Probably because Ulva hadn't given him any.

The old mayor had another question, and Tomas began to fear he'd never get any answers. "If the rumors are true, and I assume most of them are, you've been fighting a lot these last couple of years."

"True enough."

"So you've been forced to use your abilities as a host more?"

"More in the last few years than in the decade before."

"Do you feel any closer to madness?"

"Can't say I do, but I'm also always afraid that I won't be able to notice. That by the time I realize what has happened, it will be too late."

"Do you ever think about why you haven't gone mad? If you've been fighting so much lately, your theory doesn't hold much water."

Tomas stumbled over the question. He'd worried about going mad, but for some reason, he'd never questioned his basic assumptions. "I guess I haven't."

"What's a sagani?"

The sudden change of topic caught him so off guard he almost tripped over a small rock in the path. "What?"

"The sagani that wander all over the country, and the one that lives in you. What is it?"

"An animal?"

Ulva shook her head. "You know any other animal in this world that can change its shape? Any other animal that can bond with humans the way sagani do? Sagani aren't animals any more than I'm a damned plant."

Tomas withered under her assault. "I don't know. I didn't think anyone did. If anyone is getting close to an answer, it's the church. They're the ones that have been spending years trying to understand the sagani better."

Ulva scoffed. "The church! Boy, I knew you weren't the smartest man in the world the moment you stepped through my door. But right now I'm wondering if maybe this Elzeth of yours isn't the one with all the brains."

Elzeth laughed again, stirring at the compliment. "Finally, someone who understands."

"Don't need it from you, too," Tomas said to Elzeth. "He agrees, for what it's worth," he said to Ulva.

"I imagine he does. Poor creature's been trapped in there with a fool for so many years."

"I think I'm in love," Elzeth said.

Tomas shook his head, trying to clear the nonsense he was getting from both inside his head and beside him. "You two want some time alone, I'm sure we can figure something out." He said it out loud, so they could both hear him.

"Time enough for that soon," Ulva said. She pointed, and Tomas saw they were at the little cave with the nexus inside. But Tomas didn't want to proceed until he had some answers.

"What about you? Do you know what a sagani is?"

"I've got a pretty good idea. But let's go in. My bones say there's a storm on the way, and I'd rather be in there when it hits."

Tomas stubbornly stood his ground. "So, what is a sagani?"

Ulva ignored him and walked into the cave. "I'll show you everything I know, but I think it'll be easier in there."

Tomas crossed his arms.

Ulva made an exasperated sigh. "I ain't trying to be difficult. I really do believe it will be easier to show you than to explain. It should be possible at the nexus."

"Stop acting like a child," Elzeth scolded him.

Tomas almost argued, but his partner was right enough. He stepped into the cave, and the two of them stared at the glowing stone.

Ulva held out her hand.

"What, now you want my support?"

"Stop being a fool, Tomas. I've never done anything like this before, but I have the sense it will be easier if we're in physical contact. I'm going to touch the nexus, then you are.

Then, if all goes well, you'll have all the answers I can give you."

"And if it doesn't, I'll die."

"No knowledge without sacrifice," Ulva said.

Tomas stopped arguing. This was what they'd come here to do. He reached out and took Ulva's hand. She squeezed it tight, then, without further preamble, reached out and took hold of the nexus.

Tomas flinched, expecting something to happen to him, but nothing did. Maybe he felt a slight tingle in his fingers, or maybe it was just his imagination.

"Ready?" he asked Elzeth.

"Sure."

Tomas reached out for answers.

16

———

The rush of contact with the nexus was almost becoming familiar. Unending power poured through the stone into Tomas' fingers. As always, his instinctive reaction was to fight the onslaught. Strength filled tired limbs, then threatened to stretch them to bursting.

Tomas breathed out, letting the power flow through him without trying to hold onto it. The pain in his muscles eased and he felt like a leaf drifting across the top of a powerful river. The river pulled at him, but he only allowed himself to skim across the surface.

A moment later, he felt Elzeth once again. "Good to have you here," he said.

Elzeth agreed. "I don't want to say resisting the pull of the nexus is easy. But it is easier to ignore the call than before."

"Good. I'm not ready to say farewell yet." He looked around, not with his physical eyes, but with his senses, searching for some sign of Ulva.

As soon as he started the search, she appeared in front of him. She was still old, but wasn't the same age as she was in the physical world. She reached out her hand, just as she had before. This time, Tomas didn't hesitate to grasp it.

The effect was instantaneous. The nexus stopped fighting him. He felt less like an intruder and more like a guest. "You too, Elzeth," Ulva said. "Come on out."

"What?" Elzeth asked.

"As near as I can tell, we can construct our reality within the nexus. Watch." Ulva closed her eyes, and a moment later they were in a place, one now familiar to Tomas. They stood in Ulva's dining room. Tomas whistled.

"This is a place where imagination and will reign supreme," Ulva said. "Simply imagine it to be so, and it will be."

A few moments later, Tomas and Ulva were joined by a third creature. Tomas shuddered as the enormous leopard-like beast appeared. Despite knowing who it was, Tomas took a step back. The last time he'd seen Elzeth like this, Tomas had been on the brink of death, and it had been Elzeth who put him there. But he still held Ulva's hand, and she kept him from flinching too far away.

Ulva squatted down so that she was face to face with Elzeth. She reached out and ran her free hand along his spine. "Majestic."

Elzeth nuzzled against Ulva's hand like he was an oversized kitten. "I told you I liked her."

The sagani's jaw didn't move, but the voice was loud in the room. Ulva grinned, apparently hearing it, too. "You've got good taste in people, then."

"You can hear me?" Tomas wasn't sure he'd ever heard the sagani so surprised.

Ulva nodded. "Clear as if you were standing next to me. Which you are."

Tomas looked around the kitchen. If he didn't know any

better, he'd say he was actually in Ulva's kitchen. Only the physical impossibility of it kept him from believing any of this was real.

Well, that and the large sagani sitting contentedly on its haunches in the middle of the room.

Tomas fixed Ulva with a stare. "I've shown you mine. Now how about you show me yours?"

A sly grin spread across Ulva's face. She extended both her arms out and wiggled her hips.

Tomas didn't understand.

"Boy, you're as dense as a rock, aren't you?"

Tomas shrugged.

"There's no separation between me and it. I am the sagani, and it is me."

"You're in unity, right now?"

"Not sure if I'd call it unity. Hardin's described it to me, as well as a few others, and it doesn't quite match my own experience."

"How so?"

"I've heard it described as a sudden transformation, as though you go from two entities to one in a heartbeat."

Tomas agreed with the description.

"I merged with my sagani over the slow course of years. We just grew closer and closer until one day I realized that there wasn't any real difference between us. The only time I feel any separation at all is when I'm in here, and that's only the slightest of tugs. Otherwise, we might as well be one."

A year ago, Tomas might have dismissed Ulva's claim as the raving words of a host consumed by madness. But they were an eerie echo of Ghosthands' claim last autumn. The church's best killer had claimed to be the master of the sagani within. Perhaps he and Ulva had found similar paths.

It would go some way toward explaining Ghosthands' incredible skill.

Was that Tomas' path to victory?

As soon as the question occurred to him, some deep instinct in him rebelled against the idea. Unity might be the source of his greatest strength, but it came at the cost of everything that made him Tomas. "What's it like for you?"

Ulva shrugged. "Happened so slowly, I'm not even sure I could tell you the difference. I'm sure I'm a different woman than I was before, but it seems to me we're always changing anyway. Didn't figure I was losing much."

"So you still feel like...you?"

"Near as I can tell. I think it helps with aging, too. I've not been a host as long as you, but I'm not that far behind, either. Like you, I've noticed no tics, nor any odd behaviors."

Tea appeared on the table, as if it had always been there. Tomas and Ulva sat down, and Elzeth prowled around the room. Tomas looked around, still struggling to accept he was connected to the nexus. But he could feel the power around him, as though if he stepped out of the house he'd be picked up by a tornado. "Where do we start?"

"Probably best to begin with the nexuses. From there, I think the rest will make more sense." She smirked. "You mind if I change our surroundings? I find it's easier to think when I have an image before me."

"Go ahead."

Her smirk grew, and the kitchen vanished. Suddenly, Tomas was floating in a void, an endless emptiness without so much as a pinprick of light for reference. He swore, and was answered only by Ulva's laugh. A moment later, a glowing sphere appeared, smaller than a marble. It grew rapidly.

With a start, Tomas understood that it wasn't growing.

They were flying through the void, approaching it at tremendous speeds. What had appeared to be smaller than a marble was actually enormous. They stopped as it filled their whole field of view. Tomas could pick out features below. Snow-capped mountains were on his left, with enormous fields of plains and expansive forests below him. Mighty rivers carved through the land, threading their ways through valleys and fields to dump themselves into oceans and seas. He looked over at Ulva, floating beside him. "Is this our planet?"

She shrugged. "Not exactly. Some of this is my imagination. Some of it I've learned. It's close, at least."

Tomas could do little except stare. Whether a figment of Ulva's imagination or not, it was the most spectacular sight Tomas had ever seen. Ulva made a gesture with her left hand, and pale blue lights appeared. They started on Tomas' right, to the east, and spread across the land. There were hundreds of lights, twinkling like stars in the sky. Without being told, Tomas knew what they were. "The nexuses. There are so many."

"And this is where every one of them is. The geography surrounding them might be incorrect, but their relative locations are perfectly fixed. I can feel each and every one of them."

"How?"

"The only way to learn is to try it yourself. The best way I can describe it is like I'm listening to my sagani, except it's the nexus whispering to you. You're connected to one. Listen to it. Hear what it has to say, for once."

Tomas almost spit. He'd been a host longer than Ulva, and was closer to Elzeth than he'd ever been to another human. Who was she to tell him to listen?

But the vision before him, this whole experience with

the nexus, tempered his pride. His way wasn't the only way. Hells, it might not even be the best way. So he strained to hear anything.

The only sound he heard was Elzeth chuckling.

After another minute, he surrendered. He shook his head.

"Stop trying so hard," Ulva said. "True listening isn't something you achieve through force of will. It's a surrender, an openness."

Tomas glared at her but held his tongue.

"It's not all that different from when you touch the nexus. Fighting the power would destroy you. But if you let it flow through you, it allows you deeper within. Try again, but don't strain like you did before. It's not like trying to hear a whisper across a crowded room. Just empty your mind. For someone like you, that should come easy enough."

Elzeth laughed again. "We should keep her around." She scratched behind his ears.

Tomas ignored their budding friendship.

The idea of pushing thoughts from his mind was familiar enough. His sword masters had taught him much the same growing up. They'd shown him a place beyond thought. It was, they had stressed, perhaps the most important lesson they could teach. No matter the quality of one's technique, it meant nothing if thoughts and fears clouded the warrior's mind. Paradoxically, the fighter who worried the most about winning, or of living through the fight, was the one most likely to lose.

Tomas approached the task as though he was approaching a duel. He cleared all thoughts from his mind and waited. He surrendered any expectation of victory.

In time, the nexus responded.

It didn't speak to him in any way that he recognized. It was more like a physical presence. The nexus he was connected to glowed brighter, distinguishing itself on the imagined map of the world.

But there was something else, a deeper truth he hadn't uncovered yet. Hard as it was, he continued to wait without expectation. He closed his eyes. Ulva and Elzeth were speaking quietly, but their voices faded to silence as his focus narrowed.

The nexus didn't stand alone. Thin strands of power flowed from them to something deeper. Tomas followed those strands like a spider checking her web, crawling slowly forward.

Then he stumbled into a power unlike anything he'd felt before. The nexuses had always felt like a bottomless well, and now he understood why. Deep in the heart of this planet, there was a presence, indescribable in its vastness. It was awesome and terrifying in equal measure.

Ulva's voice penetrated his experience of the moment. "Now, go just a little deeper."

She sounded satisfied with what he'd accomplished, for once.

Tomas obeyed, letting himself sink. Again, he felt like a leaf on a current, but this time it felt like he had a destination. He waited, eager to see what lay ahead.

He was thrust out of the heart of the planet, propelled along one of the threads to a nexus. Tomas hit the nexus, but didn't stop. Instead, it felt as though he was divided into dozens of different viewpoints. With one eye, he flew high above the prairie. With another, he was as small as an ant, staring up at grass the same way Tomas sometimes stared up at ancient trees. He was everywhere at once. He could live like this forever, a part of all things. The idea of giving up his own limited body, for all of this, was tempting.

"Come back."

This time, it wasn't Ulva that spoke to him, but Elzeth. Tomas didn't want to return. This was something wonderful, something peaceful. It was freedom the likes of which he'd only dreamed.

But he wouldn't willingly leave Elzeth any more than the sagani would leave him. He tore himself away from what he'd discovered and found himself once again floating above the planet, next to Elzeth and Ulva.

"There's a danger to going too deep. A temptation that's hard to fight," Ulva said.

Tomas nodded. Words seemed crude to him right now.

Below him, the scene had changed. He still saw the nexuses, but now there was more detail. He saw the brightly glowing heart of the planet, and he saw the faint traces of the sagani like grains of sand covered across the land.

For the first time in his life, Tomas understood.

17

They ascended through the layers of the nexus, and Tomas again searched for that dark presence that represented his body. He found it with little difficulty, and he returned to the physical world with a surprising gentleness. It felt like he had been in a boat that bumped up softly against a pier. He let go of the nexus and looked at his hand, somewhat surprised it remained unchanged.

"Do you see?" Ulva asked.

"It's all one. The nexuses, the sagani, and whatever it is that beats at the heart of this planet."

"Perhaps you do have a bit of a brain hiding somewhere in that head of yours."

Tomas stared at the nexus. Knowing what it was made it even more impressive. Then a sudden wave of disappointment crashed over him. "It doesn't make me any stronger, though."

"Maybe not today, but with what you learned, it seems to me you'll be well on your way to solving that particular conundrum."

Tomas felt a sudden urge to reach out and caress the

nexus, to plumb its depths one more time. He knew for a fact this was his desire, not Elzeth's. He forced his hands to stay by his side. "How often have you done this?"

"A few times. I get curious and come here, seeking answers. But I try to avoid coming here too often. Every time it's the same. I never want to return, and one of these days, I think I might not. Actually considering that being the way I shuffle off this mortal coil. Once Jonasson's in a good place, maybe I'll come out here and let myself get lost in that stone."

"There are far worse ways to go." Tomas swallowed hard and took a step away from the nexus. "Don't suppose you have any idea what the church wants with them?"

"Got no answers to that one, unfortunately."

"Yeah, not sure anyone outside the church does."

Tomas turned to leave, but Ulva held him back for one moment more. "One more thing, if you'll permit an old lady to ramble on for a moment."

After what she'd shown him, he didn't have a problem with it at all.

"I'm not quite sure how, but I'm certain that whatever the nexuses are, humans are connected to them, too. Not like the sagani, of course, but connected all the same."

"You've sensed that?"

"Not like the other parts. It's more an intuition, and a bit of logic. Sagani don't make hosts of any other creature on this planet. Just us. And when we're connected to the nexus, it responds to our wills, at least to a degree. Whatever is happening, we're a part of it, too."

"Is that why you're such a pacifist? You think we matter?"

Ulva snorted. "I was a pacifist a long time before I was a host, and a long time before I even had an inkling the nexuses existed. But yes. If we're connected to all of that, I think it stands to reason that human life is valuable. Might just be the most valuable resource of all."

"I think the same, you know."

"Sure don't act like you do."

Tomas let the matter drop. He suspected they could both argue the matter until they dropped over dead and still wouldn't see eye to eye.

They began the journey back together, each lost in the silence of their own thoughts.

At the outskirts of Alliston, another question troubled Tomas. "Why haven't you taught anyone else what you know?"

"Who's to say that I haven't?"

"Have you?"

She grinned. "No."

"So why not?"

"A few reasons. The easiest excuse is because most people aren't ready to hear what I have to say. Most hosts aren't close enough with the sagani within. I think that's why touching a nexus kills most of them. In your case, Elzeth wants to stay with you, and in mine, the sagani and I have become nearly inseparable. But that isn't how it works for most people. They become a host and they're either scared of what they've become, or they get drunk on the possibilities of being a host. They burn out quick because the nature of the relationship isn't understood."

"Which seems to be all the more reason you should teach what you've learned."

"I've tried, Tomas." She came to a stop. "It took me years to learn that what I'd done was something different. It always felt natural enough to me. But when I teach it, you know what happens?"

Tomas shook his head.

"No one listens. Oh, sure, they say they do and they might make an effort. But it's hard work for most people, and there are other problems that seem bigger and more important. And so eventually they drift away. In all my years, you're the first person who's understood anything, and you're a damned fool. Of course, I think most of what makes you unique is Elzeth, so I suppose I should be thanking him."

"Elzeth?"

"Hey, don't sound so surprised," the sagani grumbled.

Ulva nodded and resumed walking. "He's different. Can't put my finger on why, exactly, and wish you two could stick around for a while longer so I could understand, but it still isn't worth the risk to the town. Still, if you can figure out a way to understand him better, it might also be a path toward that strength you crave."

They passed through the gate and into Alliston. As always, the place was a hive of activity, but everyone passing by at least offered Ulva a quick nod.

They reached Hardin's house and Ulva stepped right in.

"You kill him?" Hardin asked. He'd been less than enthused about the two of them visiting the nexus together.

"No, despite my best efforts."

Hardin came out of the kitchen into the living room to greet them. He looked them both over, as if to check their health. Satisfied, he turned most of his attention to Ulva. "We're leaving in the morning. Got a few more things to take care of here first. I'm only taking about half my first squad."

"Who you putting in charge while you're gone?"

"No one. All the other squads have plenty of work to

keep them busy, and I told them that if there was anything pressing to take it to you."

Ulva glared at him for that, but it had no effect on Hardin. After a moment, she relented. "What's your plan?"

Hardin glanced at Tomas, who answered for both of them. "Plan is maybe a strong word. We won't really know what's happening until we reach Kimson. But we'll scout it out, and if we can figure out what the church is doing, we'll stop it."

Ulva looked at Tomas as though he was the world's greatest fool. Fortunately, he was getting used to that look. "You're right. That ain't much of a plan at all."

"It's hard to plan for what we don't know," Hardin argued. "But I can promise you we'll take all of our usual precautions, as well as a few extra."

"See that you do." Ulva looked between the two of them, then focused on Hardin. "You come home safe, you hear?"

"Yes ma'am."

Then she turned to Tomas. She looked him over, hands on her hips. "You won't be returning here, no matter how this little expedition goes. But I hope you don't die."

Tomas grinned and bowed deeply. "And I'll wish you the best of luck with Jonasson."

Ulva harrumphed, then gave Tomas a quick bow of her head before turning and stomping out the door.

As far as goodbyes went, it wasn't much of one.

Once Ulva was out of earshot, though, Hardin chuckled. "You got her all worked up," he observed. "I think she likes you."

18

———

Tomas had argued against using horses, but he might as well have been shouting at a wall. His complaints about barely having recovered from the last ride were met with deaf ears.

So it was that Tomas found himself again on a horse, riding out of the forest and into the plains. Beside him, Myra, Kyle, Hardin, and Emerson rode with practiced ease. They put the morning sun behind them as they ate up the miles between Alliston and Kimson.

Of course, they didn't ride in a straight line. Hardin hadn't just been placating Ulva when they'd last spoken. He'd done even more to protect the settlements, planning a circuitous route that was at least twice as long as the most direct way.

No one uttered a word of complaint, though. The value they placed on the secrecy of their home was clear, and if this was the cost, they would pay it gladly. Tomas couldn't imagine better company for a ride, even if he wished the journey could be made on foot instead.

The same couldn't be said for Elzeth. The sagani was restless, irritable, and moody.

And that was when they weren't arguing about the decisions Tomas had made.

Elzeth grumbled, "Remind me again why we're carrying that thing."

Tomas glanced back at his saddlebag, where one of the shards of the nexus was packed tightly away. Without the casing of the crate, he felt its pull constantly, but it was a risk he'd decided was worth it. Nexuses were powerful, and it seemed foolish to completely abandon them when they were riding toward danger. Unfortunately, the proximity to the stone made Elzeth miserable.

The sagani wasn't the only one displeased by Tomas' decision. He and Hardin had argued about it before they'd left Alliston, too. Hardin recognized the possible benefits, but the risks were too great. The stones were as likely to kill the hosts as help them.

In the end, the two of them had reached a compromise neither liked. Tomas buried most of the shards in their crate. He chose a spot not far from the cave with Hardin's nexus. But he'd kept one.

He hadn't found a use for it yet. Thus far, it remained tucked away deep in his saddlebags, and the other hosts knew to stay well enough away. He and Elzeth bore the burden of the stone's presence alone.

Unfortunately, the shard wasn't their only disagreement.

"You don't think it's worth trying?" Tomas asked. "Even if that's how we defeat Ghosthands?"

"If it works, I might as well be dead. And if it doesn't, odds are we'll go mad and we both die. I'm not seeing the benefit."

"You know damn well what the benefit is. We kill Ghosthands."

"Maybe there's more to life than just killing him. Maybe I don't think that's reason enough to sacrifice my life. Besides, you're grasping at desperate ideas. There's no guarantee Ulva's methods work. You would be betting our lives on a few offhand comments Ghosthands made, plus the fact that a grandmother can still walk. It's hardly compelling evidence."

A growl escaped from the back of Tomas' throat. "Haven't figured out any other way to beat him."

"You have a nexus with you wherever you go! You almost beat him with one last time, and I'd much rather practice that than try whatever mad ideas about unity you have in mind."

Elzeth had made his position perfectly clear, and no amount of arguing back and forth persuaded him one bit. Tomas kept trying new arguments, but he might as well have been besieging a walled town by himself.

Because of their disagreements, the ride toward Kimson was even more unpleasant than it needed to be. This argument unsettled him, in a way none of their arguments had before. It took him a full day of riding to understand why.

Before, their arguments had been subjects that didn't touch the core of their personalities. They might be stuck together, but they enjoyed each other's company, for the most part. Had Elzeth been a human, Tomas liked to think they would have been friends. When Elzeth had been furious at him, after Razin, some part of Tomas had known Elzeth had the right of it.

This, though? This felt like a chasm they couldn't bridge.

They both wanted to fight the church and see Ghosthands dead, but for some reason, Elzeth wouldn't budge on their methods.

So both he and Elzeth were grouchy. The situation wasn't improved by the weather. Storm fronts moved across the prairie with frustrating regularity, gray mist draping down from dark clouds like a veil. It was never enough to drench the party, but they never had enough time to dry off, either.

After four days of riding, they were all miserable.

Conversation faded. Hardin rode at the front of the group, tall in the saddle despite the conditions. It was mid-afternoon when he held up a hand. The others all pulled to a stop, and Hardin nudged his horse a few steps forward. Then he dismounted and waved for the others to join him.

Tomas stood beside Hardin and looked around. The reason for their stop was obvious enough. From east to west, a wide trail had been marched into the prairie. There were more footprints and hoofprints than Tomas could hope to count, but he didn't need to.

Hardin made a clicking sound with his tongue. "Well, this just got more complicated."

Myra crouched down next to the tracks, squinting. "Can't make out anything useful, but there's only one animal that leaves a trail this wide."

Hardin nodded. "An army. Didn't know there was one in the area, though. Seems like something I would have heard about."

Tomas sighed. The others hadn't noticed it yet, but it had been his first thought. "Is it just me, or does it seem like this trail is heading in roughly the same direction we want to go?"

Hardin looked around, judging their position. They had been heading from south to north, so that they could approach Kimson from an oblique direction. The tracks here beat a much straighter path west. "I'm afraid so. Any guesses how old they are?"

Myra kicked at some of the tracks. "Maybe a day or so. Not much more, for sure."

"Should we follow?" Tomas asked. He couldn't guess what an army was doing out here, nor did he really know what relations were like between the church and the army.

Hardin thought for a moment. "No. They aren't that far ahead of us, and I'd much rather not run into their rearguard if I can help it." When he saw that Tomas was about to object he held up his hand. "But we will pick up our pace. If there's an advantage to be found here, we'll use it."

The appearance of the tracks sparked the whispered conversations that the rains had doused. Speculation ran rampant among the group, but there was too little information. All that could be said for sure was that there was an army in the area, and it sure as hell looked like it was heading in the direction of Kimson.

The big question was one no one spoke out loud. Was the army here to attack Kimson, or to ally with it?

A lot rode on the answer, but Tomas couldn't guess one way or the other.

Hardin was true to his word, though. They pushed the pace, and their horses ate up the miles.

The sudden gunshots made Tomas jump. They weren't aimed at him. He heard no bullet, and as far as his eye could see, the horizon was clear. But they were closer than he'd expected. The land here rose and fell like enormous, gentle waves, and it sounded as though the shots had come from behind the next rise.

Tomas didn't even have time to wonder if they would hide from the shots or ride toward them. Before the last echo of the blast had faded, Hardin gestured them forward, and he led the charge toward battle.

19

More gunshots followed the first, echoing across the prairie as they reached the top of the rise. The shots came from different directions, confirming Tomas' suspicion they had stumbled upon a small battle. He couldn't guess how many people were involved, but he guessed there were no more than three or four rifles.

Still, that was a lot of firepower they were riding towards. Beside him, Kyle grabbed his massive bow, and for a moment Tomas almost felt sorry for whoever they found. They crested the rise at a gallop and Tomas got his first look at the battle below.

It wasn't much, as far as battles went. Given the number of rifles, Tomas had expected to see at least a few dozen people involved. A quick glance revealed less than six.

To his west, two rifles fired. Tomas' eyes tracked toward the sound, and he saw movement in the grass. Two snipers lay prone, their rifles and attention aimed at the draw below.

An army scouting group had the misfortune of being in that draw. Five riders had let their horses drink from a small stream that trickled through the bottom of the draw. They scrambled for cover, but their ambushers had caught them out in the open. If the snipers had any skill at all, this battle would be over in less than a minute.

Tomas understood what was happening easily enough. His assessment of the situation took no more than a few seconds. But figuring out *why* it was happening was a much harder task. The last time he'd checked, the church and the army were pretty much on the same side. Tomas didn't care much for either organization, and so he wasn't sure which side he wanted to help.

No small part of him just wanted to sit back and let them kill each other.

Hardin was more decisive. He turned his horse around and rode back down the same rise he just ascended. The others followed suit, putting the battle behind them. Once they were out of sight, Hardin angled west. Then he shouted his orders. "We're going to kill those ambushers. Kyle, there's a good chance we're going to be counting on you."

Kyle nodded, clutching his giant bow closer to his side.

Hardin's route kept them low, out of sight of the rise where the ambushers lay. They circled around so they could attack the snipers from the west, a journey that took them a few minutes. Tomas heard a few more shots, but then the world fell quiet once more.

Hardin completed his wide loop, and they rode toward where they'd last seen the snipers. The shooters had been near the top of the rise, but on the east face. If they remained in position, Tomas and the others would be out of sight until it was too late for the shooters to react. The same would be true if the snipers wandered down into the draw to check their kills.

Unfortunately, the shooters chose a third way. Either

they'd been satisfied by their work or they had spotted Hardin and the others when they'd first come into view. Whatever the reason, they were beating a hasty retreat from the rise, fleeing west. It gave the snipers a clear view of Hardin's group charging toward them.

Tomas expected them to turn tail and run, hopeless as the idea might be. But they displayed an extraordinary amount of composure. They gestured toward the approaching riders and held a brief discussion. Then they ran a few steps back toward the top of the rise and took kneeling positions.

Tomas would have done much the same in their place. On foot, they didn't have many choices, but taking the high ground gave them the most defensible point in the area.

He felt exposed on his horse's back. He'd never been a part of the cavalry. He'd known expert riders who claimed to feel a sort of unity with their mount, riders who believed they became something greater when working together with a horse. Tomas wasn't like that, though. Given the chance, he always preferred to have his own feet on the ground. He'd rather crawl through the grass like a snake than lead a charge.

But Hardin and the others didn't share his opinion. They charged the high ground, even though it seemed to Tomas to be the height of foolishness.

Say one thing for the strategy, though: it meant the battle would be decided quickly. Hardin galloped toward the snipers with reckless abandon, and the fight would be decided in the next minute.

The rifles fired as soon as the riders were in range. It only took a pair of shots for Tomas to realize these shooters were far more accurate than the guards of the caravan they had attacked. One bullet whined past Tomas' side, and

Myra jerked as though she was a marionette having her strings pulled. She roared in pain but didn't lose her seat. She wrapped the reins tight in her right hand, then urged her horse forward faster.

Hardin angled his horse, hoping to make the shot more difficult as they hit the beginning of the rise. The sinking feeling in Tomas' stomach grew stronger as more bullets narrowly missed. They were closing fast, but they were still too far away for Kyle and his massive bow.

Tomas tracked the movement of the rifle barrels, and when he saw one swiveling towards him, he turned his horse out of the way. Unfortunately, the muzzle tracked him without a problem. Before he could turn the horse away again, the rifle fired. Tomas braced for the impact, but it wasn't him that took the bullet. His horse shifted underneath him, and warm blood sprayed against his arm. It wasn't much in the way of warning, but it was enough. Tomas pulled his boots from the stirrups. The horse galloped valiantly for another few steps before collapsing over its front legs.

Elzeth flared to life and Tomas did nothing to fight momentum or gravity. The collapsing horse threw him forward, and all he did was tuck his arms in and grit his teeth. He hit the ground hard, tumbling and rolling until he finally skidded to a stop in the tall grass. Then he rolled onto his back and took a moment to just stare at the sky.

He felt like someone had taken a mallet and hammered it up and down his body, but as near as he could tell, nothing was broken. Elzeth had given him strength early enough in the fall that it had kept his injuries to nothing more severe than bumps and bruises. He lay there, catching his breath and debating what to do next.

Then he remembered the shard of the nexus back in the

saddlebag. He rolled over onto his stomach, then crawled back to where his horse lay. He kept close to the ground. Behind him, more gunshots echoed. He risked poking his head above the grass for a moment. He looked back just in time to see Kyle release an arrow. The distance still seemed impossibly far, but if Tomas had learned anything during the attack on the caravan, it was to not doubt the young archer.

The riders were well past him, though. Satisfied there was nothing he could do to change the course of the battle, Tomas resumed crawling toward the horse. He was by its side in a moment.

Tragic as the animal's death was, it was clear that it had at least been quick. Its glassy eyes stared into the mystery that was on the other side of the gates.

Tomas rummaged through his saddlebags, removing his pack that held the shard of the nexus. He checked quickly to make sure everything was in place after the fall, then slipped it on. He crawled a ways away from the horse and then poked his head up once again to check on the state of the battle. It was only when he did that he realized the gunshots had stopped. He popped his head up to see what was happening.

Hardin rode slowly back down the hill, weaving his horse back and forth, searching the grass for him. The man's sharp eyes didn't miss Tomas' gopher impression, and a relieved smile spread across his face. "You hurt?"

"Nothing serious. Horse is dead, though."

"It shall be missed, but right now I'm just glad it wasn't you." He rode up next Tomas "Care for a ride?"

"I think I'll stick to my feet for a moment if you don't mind."

Hardin dismounted, and together the two of them

walked toward the rise where the snipers had made their last stand.

"I'm afraid I missed most of the battle. What happened?"

"Kyle."

Nothing more needed to be said. They reached the top of the rise where Kyle, Myra, and Emerson were already studying the corpses. Myra had a bandage around her left shoulder and was a little pale. But she otherwise looked okay. Tomas was relieved. If Hardin's greater scheme was going to succeed, she was perhaps one of the most valuable assets at his disposal. No one could train others the way she trained them.

As Tomas and Hardin approached, Emerson gave the report. "Kyle killed them pretty dead, sir. Not much we can tell about them except that they're definitely from the church." He used his toe to point out the embroidered symbols on their shoulders.

Hardin and Tomas both took a turn examining the bodies, but they found nothing worth noticing. They'd been snipers, and good ones at that. That they were associated with the church came as no surprise.

Hardin gestured down to the bottom of the draw where the unfortunate army scouts had been. "Well, let's head down there. Perhaps there we'll figure out why the church and the army are suddenly trying to kill each other."

20

Tomas was a little surprised that Hardin left the rifles behind. Even though his hosts were trained in sword and bow, the rifles were still powerful weapons. They'd provide a useful defense for Alliston. Failing that, they were still expensive and would fetch a high price in many corners of the frontier.

When he asked about it, Hardin spit on the ground and glared at the weapons. "There will probably come a day, if I live long enough, that I'll have to allow those into Alliston. But I'll be damned if it'll happen one day sooner than it absolutely needs to."

Tomas almost argued the point. Personally, he felt very much the same, but with something as important to the future as Alliston was, perhaps it was time to put aside their own personal prejudices.

Hardin waved the group forward, but Myra reached out and grabbed Tomas' hand. At a look from her, Tomas let the others start down the hill without him.

Myra leaned close and spoke softly. "Best you not make a suggestion like that again. You know about his wife?"

Tomas nodded.

"When she killed herself, she did it with a rifle. I'm sure he disliked them before, but nothing like he does now."

"If Alliston is going to have a future, he's going to need rifles at some point in time. They become more widespread with every passing year, and not even being a host can protect you from a bullet."

"He knows."

Tomas shrugged. He supposed there wasn't all that much more to say. He fought for Alliston today, but its future, ultimately, was out of his hands. Ulva had made sure of that. Myra let him go and they caught up quickly to the others.

The small draw before them was quiet. As near as Tomas could tell, nothing moved down there but the horses, which were content to drink from the stream while they waited for orders that would never come.

As they descended, Tomas tried to imagine a story that would explain the ambush that had just taken place. He couldn't claim to be the most informed on current events, but the church and the army had been tentative allies, at least, since the end of the war. The church provided the government the illusion of having a moral center, and the government tended to look the other way as the church purged society of hosts. Perhaps the two organizations weren't exactly fast friends, but the arrangement had proved beneficial for both sides. Why would they endanger that? The two of them had comfortably shared power for years now.

But then again, hadn't that been part of Ghosthands' rationale for staging the Chesterton Massacre? The assassin had argued that the church needed a rallying point, something to stave off the threats that threatened them both from without and from within. At the time, Tomas had thought it was mostly empty talk, the ravings of a devout believer who saw enemies wherever he looked.

But if there was some truth the matter, well, that gave Tomas his first real sense of hope for the future in years. Despite his appeal to Hardin, he knew there was nothing he could do that would prove to be anything more than a temporary impediment to the church. But if he could somehow serve as the wedge that forced those two monstrous powers into open conflict…

His imagination danced at the possibilities. Perhaps this way there would be a future for hosts. One where they didn't have to hide or fear for their lives.

They reached the bottom of the draw, and Tomas' surge of excitement was muted. The scene in front of him reminded him of the potential cost of that future. It might be more hopeful for hosts, but there was a real danger the future he hoped for cost more than he was willing to bear.

The scouting party was as army-standard as it was possible to be. There were five bodies. Tomas knew from his own experiences that two pairs of soldiers would be low-rank enlisted, probably younger recruits who had been skilled at hunting and tracking back home. They'd be commanded by one officer. Tomas came upon the officer first, and it looked as though he had first attracted the attention of the snipers. Further on, the shooters had only spared one bullet per soldier, but here, two had done the job. They'd wanted him dead first.

Killing officers first was a common enough tactic, but again, it said something about the training of the snipers. Combined with their decision to stand and defend the rise, Tomas smelled a history of military training. Though there had only been two rifles against five scouts, the scouts never had a chance. They'd only carried one rifle among the five of them.

Up ahead, one of the corpses suddenly moved, and every host in Hardin's party prepared for battle.

There was no need. One of the soldiers had been shot in the gut, but it hadn't killed him yet. It was a fatal wound for someone who wasn't a host, and Tomas saw no sagani nearby. The young man hadn't even had time to draw his sword once the rifles started tearing apart his unit.

Tomas hurried toward the injured man, kneeling next to him before the others arrived. "What happened?" Tomas asked.

Speaking didn't come easily, but the scout coughed out a reply as blood filled his lungs. "We were out on patrol. Never had any idea they were there. Figure it was the church, but never saw for sure."

Tomas grimaced. The young man didn't have long, and he had to know something useful. "Why would the church attack you?"

The scout answered right away. "Something in Kimson they don't want anyone to know about. Something that would give them too much power. Command wouldn't say what, but we figured some sort of weapon."

A weapon? It certainly fit with what Tomas already knew. It would explain the piles of steel they'd taken from the caravan. And if the church had somehow found a way for it to be powered by a nexus, that would explain the shards. It still didn't explain the knights, but if the rumors of a weapon were being taken seriously enough that the government would send an army out, Tomas was willing to believe them.

He suspected that was all he would get from the unfortunate soldier, but he pushed a little harder. "Any last requests? Anything you want me to pass on to your commander?"

"Kill them. Make them pay for what they're trying to do."

The vitriol in the request caught Tomas off guard. He swallowed the lump in his throat. Then he reached out and clasped the dying man's hand. "We will."

The scout nodded and then rested. The last of the fight went out of his body and Tomas felt the moment that he died as his hand went slack. Tomas took the time to say the old words over the scout.

When he looked up, he was surrounded by all the others. They'd heard everything, which saved Tomas from having to repeat it.

Hardin grunted. "If the church and the army are threatening war, we've got a whole different situation on our hands."

Tomas stood. He had an idea, and for once he didn't think it was half bad. "If the church and the army want a war," he said, "I think we should give them one."

21

____

"What exactly did you have in mind?" Harding asked.

"Strong as we might be, there's only so much the five of us can do against the church. But maybe we don't have to do as much as we think. I don't suppose y'all have heard the stories of the time I destroyed a town, have you?"

Everyone nodded as though he'd asked a foolish question. Of course they had.

Tomas couldn't help but feel a little dismayed. Elzeth chose that exact moment to rub dirt in the wound. "Bet this wasn't what you thought about back when you were still concerned about leaving a legacy," he said.

"No, it most certainly was not." As much as Elzeth's words cut at him, Tomas was glad to hear some semblance of the sagani's sharp wit return. He'd missed it the last few days.

He returned his attention to the group. "I'm not sure what version you heard—"

That opened the floodgates. Before he could finish his

thought, Emerson interrupted him. "I heard you killed two squads of knights on your own."

Myra shook her head. "It was only one squad, as well as a whole branch of the Family."

Hardin scratched at his chin. "I heard you wrestled with a sagani on fire, and that was what destroyed the town."

Tomas looked at all of them, astounded. "What?"

Hardin shrugged. "I mean, I didn't believe it, but the guy telling me the story sure did."

Tomas pressed his palms into his eyes. Then he shook his head. None of it mattered. "To keep a long story short, when I came into town the church and the Family were fighting over it. And yes, a squad of knights did die, but it was only because I was able to turn the feud that was already brewing between the two sides into an all-out fight. That was what killed the knights and destroyed the town."

They looked disappointed there wasn't more to the story. Their expressions made Tomas want to shake them awake. He couldn't be the hero they expected him to be, especially when their expectations were based in stories that had no truth to them.

Hardin was the first to recover. "So, that's what you propose to do here?"

"Same general idea, and it might not be that hard. The church is clearly ready to kill to protect whatever they're working on in Kimson. And the government sent an army all the way out here to deal with the problem. Everything is set for us. All we need to do is make sure we give them that little push over the edge."

"And how exactly do you plan on pulling that off?"

Tomas considered the question. Truth be told, he hadn't really thought his idea through before announcing it. "I suppose the first thing we'll need is to get the lay of the land, figure out what the leadership of the church and the army are thinking."

Myra shook her head. "You thinking you're going to march up and just ask them?"

"No. I think for now our plan remains mostly the same. We scout the area and find out all we can. Then we start making decisions."

"You want to find that army trail and follow it?" Hardin asked. "I can't imagine they're much more than a day ahead of us."

"I think it's best to start with Kimson. It's the center of everything, and we need to know what it's looking like. I've got more questions there than with the army."

Hardin considered it for a moment. "I suppose it's as good a plan as any. Like you say, it's not really all that different than what we were thinking about doing already." He looked around the circle. "Any thoughts or suggestions?"

Tomas liked that Hardin gave the others a chance to weigh in. In fact, he liked most everything about Hardin's leadership. He had the courage to take risks and the wisdom to know he couldn't accomplish his missions alone.

If Hardin had any weakness, it was his willingness to charge headlong into battles without second thought. Tomas supposed it was the very aspect of Hardin's character that caused others to look up to him, but it made Tomas uneasy.

Call him a coward, but Tomas had always preferred the quieter routes to victory. He liked to sneak up on enemies from behind, or pit them against one another. In his opinion, the only time to charge straight at an enemy was when they'd left you no other choice.

The others had nothing to add, so they once again mounted their horses. Tomas took hold of one of the horses that had been drinking from the stream. It looked friendly enough.

Hardin consulted his maps and informed them Kimson was about seven miles away. That caused Tomas to glance back at the resting place that had been the scouting unit's final stop.

Kyle was the one who gave voice to Tomas' worries. "A bit concerning if the church is setting ambushes this far out of town. Makes me a little nervous about what we're going to encounter as we get closer."

Hardin stared at the map, tracing his finger along a route. "Agreed. This might have been in response to the army, though. Guessing they're trying to keep a low profile by avoiding the road, but it's hard to hide an advance of that size. I was going to approach Kimson from the north, but with the army heading that direction now I'm thinking we ride around to the south and approach that way. Best we stay away from any armies until we know more."

Again, there were no complaints, and Tomas endured another long bit of riding. He took comfort in knowing it would soon be over. He was almost ready to be shot at again, if only it meant no more time on a horse. They crossed the trail of the army once again, but it provided them no more information than they'd gotten from it earlier.

Their pace was slow enough to allow every eye to remain glued to their surroundings. If there were other believers with rifles waiting to ambush them, Hardin and his crew would have very little warning. The glint of sunlight off of a barrel might be the only sign they were riding into trouble.

At one point, Hardin fell back to talk to Tomas. "You got any specific ideas for when we reach Kimson?"

"If it looks safe to approach, I assumed some or all of us

could just walk right in. Well, probably just some of you, being as my face is a little well-known these days."

Hardin's eyes went wide.

Tomas shrugged. "No one knows we're hosts. We can ride in, claiming to be a survey party for a new settlement. It's close enough to the truth, I suppose. We spend a day talking to people, and by the time we leave, we should have a pretty good idea what they're thinking."

Hardin gave him a sideways look. "So, you're telling me that you want us, a group of hosts, to ride into a place that will almost certainly hang us if they find out what we are? And then you want us to stay there, even as we know an army is approaching and the church is building some powerful weapon?"

Tomas scratched at his chin. "Well, when you put it like that, it sounds like a pretty bad idea."

"Could be that it is a bad idea. I think I'm starting to see how it is you end up getting in so much trouble wherever you go."

"Elzeth keeps saying the same thing."

"Sounds like we might get along." Hardin considered Tomas' proposal for a bit. Then he sighed. "The worst part of it is, it might still be the best idea we got. Somehow I have the feeling we won't be able to learn enough by just sitting outside the town with a looking glass."

Another small squall passed overhead as they finished their ride. According to Hardin's map, they were close. Kimson was located on the northern shore of a small lake. Coming from the south, Hardin and the others were able to keep the lake between them and the settlement.

The group dismounted out of sight of the town, and Emerson and Kyle volunteered to stay back with the horses as Tomas, Myra, and Hardin hiked toward a place where they could take their first look. It wasn't long before Kimson's walls came into view. They crouched down. Hardin pulled out his looking glass, and Tomas did the same.

Hardin took one look and swore. "Think we're going to need to consider a new plan," he said. Without another word, he handed the glass to Myra.

Tomas focused on the town a moment later. He swore, too.

Kimson was a small place, no more than a couple of dozen houses at most. Walls had been built around the west, east, and north sides, leaving only the south side open. But to get there, one had to cross the lake, an approach that would be easily observed even at night.

More to the point, though, half a dozen guards stood at the front gate. Two dogs on long leashes roamed back and forth, never leaving the gate far behind. The dogs would only be there for one reason: to identify visitors as hosts. Hardin and his crew would be marked before they even made it to the gate. And there wasn't any point in sneaking in. If the town was that small, there'd be no hiding in a crowd.

Tomas studied the town for a bit more, then collapsed his looking glass. "Well, the front door is definitely out."

"If they're concerned enough to have dogs on watch, I wouldn't be surprised if there were at least a handful more within," Hardin said.

"Not even sure that matters," Tomas said. "I don't see any way to sneak in, and even if we did, the first person to spot us would know we don't belong. Place is smaller than I was expecting."

"Same." Hardin agreed. "So, any ideas what we do next?"

Tomas shook his head. The only idea that came to mind

wasn't a good one. "Care to pay a visit to our friends in the army?"

Hardin grunted. "I retired for a reason. But don't see what else we can do." He stood up wearily. "Well, let's get to it."

22

———

Much to Tomas' dismay, the decision to find the army meant yet another ride on the horse.

He didn't mind the animals. Far from it. He always tried to befriend the creatures, especially if they were being kind enough to carry him from place to place. But ever since he'd become a host, he'd much preferred to walk. He liked the feel of his feet after a long day of walking, and he noticed more about his surroundings. Most people felt different, especially considering the much longer distances the average person could cover on horseback. But to Tomas, there was something deeply satisfying about walking the land.

He didn't complain, though. This next ride took them through the darkest part of the night, after the sun had set and before Tolkin rose. They didn't follow the tracks of the army, concerned they might encounter the rearguard by accident. Instead, they once again crossed the army's trail, circling the long way around so they could come at the army from the north.

When they saw the first flickers of campfires off in the

distance, they rode even farther away. It would do them no good to be found by one of the army's scouting parties, especially if word of the ambushed unit had spread.

Tomas realized it would reflect on them even more poorly if it was discovered he was riding an army horse. In his experience, nothing made one look more guilty than riding on a horse stolen from a dead man.

They found a small grove of trees. This time, Myra and Emerson stayed behind with the horses while Tomas, Kyle, and Hardin worked their way toward the camp. Kyle could protect them at range while Tomas and Hardin observed the army.

The three of them progressed slowly, crouching to blend in with the tall grass. Elzeth simmered in Tomas' stomach, granting him sharper vision and hearing. With both moons high in the sky, there was plenty of light to see by, and he was confident he would spot scouts before they spotted him.

It ended up being true enough. About halfway to the army's encampment, Tomas spotted a group of soldiers on patrol. The three hosts sat patiently in the grass as the scouts passed a few hundred feet to the south. Only when Hardin thought they were safe did the group continue.

Another half hour of sneaking brought them close enough to the camp to study it with their looking glasses. Tomas' first impressions weren't optimistic. Like Kimson, the army unit was patrolled both by humans and dogs. The coverage wasn't as complete as around the church settlement, but it was enough that Tomas had no desire to test it.

He felt Hardin's disappointment as his own. He'd been hoping for some easy way to approach the camp, but there wouldn't be one. Being a host, which so often worked in his favor, now made it almost impossible to get the information he sought. He noticed, too, that both the army and the church were making efforts to protect themselves against hosts, specifically.

He kept studying the camp, looking for some way to move forward. Then he barked a soft laugh when he saw the banners.

"Care to tell me what's so funny?" Hardin asked.

"That's the 34th."

"And?"

"I've had a run-in with them before. Their general and I got along well enough. There's a chance he and I might be able to talk." Almost as soon as he spoke, he realized the mistake in his reasoning. "Of course, that happened back before I became one of the most wanted criminals in the country."

He dredged up the memories of that prior meeting. He and General Gavan had parted on good terms. It was worth a try. "I'm happy to arrange a meeting, if you can't think of anything better."

Hardin looked like Tomas had asked him to swallow a bug. "How certain are you that he'll meet you?"

"A little? He might also send the whole army after me. And that's assuming he's still in charge. He was getting up in years the last time I saw him."

"Do you even listen to yourself when you're making a plan?"

"Probably not as closely as I should."

Hardin shook his head and studied the camp. "It's not that it's impossible to get in there. But it's too risky, especially if all we're looking for is information. How would you arrange your meeting with this general?"

"Can't stroll in, I suppose. I'd probably ambush one of

the scouting parties and have them deliver a message for me."

Hardin sounded as though he'd choked on something. "You are a very unique man, Tomas. Not sure I could handle having you around too much, though. Something tells me I'd either go mad trying to reason out your plans or get myself killed by blindly following them." He sighed. "I don't want to risk my people over such a harebrained scheme."

"Then don't. It's probably for the best anyway, as your presence would just lead to more questions I don't want to have to answer. I'll ambush the scout group alone, and then you'll have nothing to worry about."

"Except you getting captured and tortured."

"Give me a little credit. One scout group won't be a problem."

Hardin didn't give his final answer for some time. Tomas suspected he was searching for a more reasonable way to learn what they needed. Only problem was, he wasn't going to find one. Finally, Hardin acknowledged it as well. "Fine. Just make sure nothing can be traced back to us."

And that was how Tomas found himself out on the prairie alone, with only Elzeth and the moons to keep him company. After all the riding and time with others, Tomas found the solitude refreshing.

He liked others well enough, and there were times he craved company. But others also made life more complicated, and his life wasn't one that needed more complications. Besides, he had Elzeth, so he was never truly alone.

He was grateful for Elzeth tonight. Success required

sharper senses, and the sagani continued to simmer deep within.

It would have been easier if the 34th's scouts would have followed some sort of pattern, but they wandered around aimlessly, making it hard to predict when and where he would find one of the units. Setting an ambush was likewise difficult because he couldn't always predict their routes. Once he thought he'd found a perfect location, only for the unit to turn away before reaching him.

Time was starting to become an enemy. Before long the sun would rise, making his ambush that much more difficult. For this to work, he had to strike fast enough he wouldn't have to engage in a longer fight. Injuries, a general could overlook. But if soldiers died, Tomas might as well hop back on the horse and ride as far away from here as he could. Or knot his own noose to save General Gavan some time.

He spotted movement to his east. A group of five scouts roamed through the grass, moving slowly. It might have been caution that slowed their steps, but Tomas suspected weariness. The night was coming to a close and they would be eager for their relief come dawn.

Once again, Tomas said a silent thanks to Elzeth. The sagani kept him awake and alert.

He crouched and walked a little farther south. Once he was in their path, he rested on his knees and waited for them to come to him.

And this time, they did. They passed within ten feet of him, and their shuffling steps and half-lidded eyes told Tomas all he needed to know. He waited until they were past him, then exploded from his hiding place. Elzeth burned bright, and Tomas delivered powerful blows to the pair of scouts who guarded the rear. They collapsed, clutching at their stomachs as they gasped for air.

Tomas stepped past them. The other pair of enlisted scouts turned toward him, and he kicked one in the stomach. She doubled over, and Tomas put her out of mind. The last of the enlisted scouts tried to draw his sword, but Tomas was too close. Tomas placed his hand on the bottom of the sword's hilt and slammed it back into its sheath before it cleared. The scout looked up in surprise, and never saw Tomas' knee as it, too, claimed a victim.

The officer, displaying some of the training that had made the army so dangerous, reacted well. She carried a rifle, and it was already coming up by the time Tomas worked his way through the others. Tomas spun and kicked, knocking the rifle's muzzle away from him.

His momentum carried him to the officer. She reversed the direction of the muzzle, but gripped the rifle tightly, swinging it back at him like it was the world's most expensive club. Tomas caught it and twisted it out of her hands.

She barely faltered at the loss of the weapon. Before he had the chance to throw it to the side, she attacked him with a jab to his nose. Tomas tilted his head to the side, then kicked straight out at her. She was too focused on his hands, and never saw it coming. It forced her back a few paces, giving Tomas time to control the situation. He tossed the rifle far enough away that it wouldn't be a worry, then advanced.

She swung halfheartedly at him, but he shrugged the blow off. "I'm just here to talk," he said.

She stumbled back a step and swung again at him. He twisted around, drawing a knife from his belt and holding it lightly to her throat.

That, finally, caught her attention. She stilled.

"Thank you. Would you be so kind as to order your scouts to give us a bit of room? I don't like crowded spaces."

The others were coming to their feet, and it wouldn't be long before they drew their swords and forced Tomas into that fight he was hoping to avoid.

"Why should I?" the woman snarled.

"Besides being the first to die?"

He had to give her high marks for courage, because she didn't utter a syllable to help him. He sighed. "I'd like to think that it's obvious I could have killed all of you had I wanted. You'll notice, though, that all of you are alive and mostly well. I really do just want to talk."

"Then talk."

"I converse much better when I'm certain I'm not going to have to fight at any given moment. I don't want to hurt anyone, but I will if it comes to that."

The officer saw reason. "Back up, y'all. He says he means us no harm. And if he's lying, I imagine there's no place on this prairie that'll be safe from the 34th's wrath."

The soldiers hesitated for a moment, but the chain of command remained strong. They gave short bows and backed up. "Satisfied?" the officer asked.

"I am, thank you." Tomas decided to match the cooperation with a gesture of his own. He sheathed the knife and stepped away from her. He didn't drop his guard, but he appreciated the chance for them to speak face to face.

"So, you went to an awful lot of trouble. What do you want to say?"

"Is General Gavan still in charge of the 34th?"

"Until the day his soul crosses onto the other side of the gates."

That was a relief. All of this would have been for nothing

if he'd retired. But Tomas had suspected he still was. Gavan seemed like a man who would die in his command, either on a battlefield or behind his desk.

He dug into a pocket and took out a letter. He'd penned it earlier, keeping it deliberately vague. It wasn't sealed, as he hadn't the supplies, but he expected Gavan would understand the meaning well enough. He handed it to her. "I'd like you to take this to him, please."

"Why?"

"Because I think I can help him with Kimson, and because I'm an ally worth having. But all I'm asking is that you deliver it to him personally."

"That's it?"

"That's it."

"What if I read the letter first and decide it's not something I like?"

"Then do as you will. But I think he would at least like to see it. We're old acquaintances."

"I find that hard to believe."

Tomas shrugged. "Regardless."

It wasn't much, but he hoped it was enough. He retreated slowly, watching to ensure none of the recovering soldiers went for their weapons. Then he faded into the darkness, hoping he hadn't brought a whole army down on him.

23

———

Tomas waited in a small grove of trees, just as he'd promised in his note to Gavan. He was alone, and hadn't had any contact with Hardin or the others since he'd left to ambush the scouting unit. They weren't taking any risks they could avoid.

The waiting was irritating, but he imagined it was worse for Hardin and the others. Because they didn't dare risk communicating, they had arranged everything to unfold based on elapsed time. Tomas had been given one night to make contact with the scouts, and one full day to wait for Gavan. If Tomas' plan hadn't worked by then, Hardin would consider the attempt a failure.

On one hand, the time wasn't much. It would allow Myra to heal fully from her injury and give the others time to rest. But in a land crawling with both the church and the 34th, a day of hiding and waiting would carry enough stresses of its own. At the top of Tomas' mind, if something went wrong, it would be a full day before Hardin and the others would know to worry.

Tomas suspected that part didn't matter all that much. If

he was captured, Hardin and the others would do whatever seemed best for them, and that seemed unlikely to include Tomas. They wouldn't worry overmuch about his fate. Tomas wasn't one of them, and he'd known the risks when he proposed this scheme.

He tapped his fingers against his thighs, and though he tried to sit still and meditate, he couldn't find the focus. If he wasn't thinking about the church and army, he was thinking about the nexuses and Ulva. He spent most of his time pacing the trees restlessly, always keeping an eye on the southern horizon.

There were a lot of ways for this plan to fail, and not so many ways for it to work out well.

He paced faster. He didn't mind the risk, but he hated waiting. If the inquisitors ever caught him again, they'd break him faster if they just left him in a room with nothing to do.

A little after noon, a single horse appeared on the horizon. From this distance, Tomas couldn't tell who it was. His breath caught as he waited to see if the rider approached alone.

The rider pulled out a looking glass and pointed it straight at the trees. Tomas emerged and gave a little wave. The small grove was enough to offer him some measure of cover in case the army came with rifles, but was too small to hide any force of significance. The rider didn't respond to Tomas' gesture. The figure watched for a while longer, then turned and disappeared over the horizon.

"That doesn't bode well," Elzeth said.

Tomas waited. What was done was done. Like the snipers on the hill, there was no point in him running. It was the middle of the day, and if they'd come to kill him they would have brought rifles, dogs, and fast horses. Fleeing did nothing but prolong the inevitable.

A few minutes later another rider appeared. The rider's uniform was different, brighter than the drab green outfits that most soldiers wore. This rider didn't stop to observe Tomas, but rode forward, sitting tall in the saddle. Even from a distance, the aura of command that surrounded him was obvious. Had they been on opposite sides of a battlefield, Tomas would have had no trouble searching for him, no matter what uniform he wore.

The sight of General Gavan was the first hint that Tomas' mad plan might just work. There were still plenty of ways for everything to go sideways, but the fact the general was riding alone gave Tomas hope.

The general rode at a measured pace, and as he neared, Tomas saw the way his eyes roamed over the trees. He pulled to a stop about ten steps away from Tomas, looked around one last time, then fixed his stare on Tomas.

"Good to see you again, sir," Tomas said.

Gavan grunted, then exhaled sharply. He dismounted, the motion still smooth and easy despite his age. The general had more gray in his hair than the last time they'd crossed paths, and the wrinkles around his eyes had deepened, but he still moved like he was ready for a fight. "If I'd had the slightest clue the trail of destruction you were going to leave behind, you'd never have left my camp alive," Gavan said.

As far as introductions went, it was worse than what Tomas had hoped for, but it wasn't as bad as it could have been. He was still out here, and Tomas hadn't caught sight of a sniper yet. "If I'd known, I might have let you."

Gavan's eyes narrowed. "What do you want?"

"To help you stop whatever's happening in Kimson."

"You mean you want my help, just like you did back then."

Tomas shrugged. "It's all the same, I suppose."

"Why would I?"

A fair question. Gavan had a competent army at his back and a mission to fulfill. All Tomas had was educated guesses. Fortunately, he liked to gamble. "Whatever the church is building, they don't want anyone near. They've already killed one of your scouting groups, and that was in an ambush."

Gavan stopped him. "You know that? What happened?"

"I came upon the scout group in a draw a few miles east of here. Two snipers ambushed them."

"We found them," Gavan said, looking into the trees again for hidden troops. "The snipers were killed with a bow."

Tomas kept his face blank. "The point is, the church isn't going to let you get near Kimson without a fight. It's well protected, with people who know what they're doing. And they have knights who've become hosts. Not to mention this weapon everyone is whispering about. You're looking at a bloody fight, but if you let me help, maybe it's a little less bloody for you."

"Where are your friends?"

Tomas had worried that talking about the scouting group would get him in trouble. But there was nothing for it now. The last card was about to be drawn, so he might as well go all in on his hand. "Hiding, a ways away. Figured this was something better done alone."

"What kind of help did you bring?"

"A few hosts. People who don't like what the church is doing, and really don't like the idea of the church getting its hand on new weapons."

Gavan chewed on his lower lip and looked away from Tomas. "You said something about host knights?"

"Yes, sir. Fought a few a while back. They were on their way here, which was what got our attention."

"You're saying that *knights* are becoming hosts now?"

"Doesn't make any sense to us, either, sir. It's why I'm here. Why we're here."

"Even if I did want your help, there's the small problem of you being the most wanted man in the country right now."

"Because I've been fighting the church. Which is exactly what you're here to do."

"Was Chesterton about fighting the church?"

There it was again, the one sin no one would ever forgive. The act that stained his hands with blood that wouldn't wash off. But he also saw that if he didn't have an answer, Gavan wouldn't cooperate.

To claim it had all been Ghosthands' manipulation might have been true, but it was also an excuse. One he couldn't hide behind.

He couldn't come up with an explanation that would satisfy Gavan.

He didn't try. "I believe my actions at Chesterton were justified," Tomas said as he forced himself to meet Gavan's gaze. "But that doesn't mean I don't regret them. If I had a chance to go back and live that night over again, I would like to find another way. But the responsibility for my actions is my own."

Gavan considered for a long time. But when he sighed, Tomas knew they had a chance. "Life would be a lot easier for me if I didn't believe you," he said. "But I do, and if they have hostile knights that are hosts, then I might just need someone like you."

Tomas gave Gavan a sharp bow. "You won't regret this, sir."

Gavan handed Tomas a pass from one of his pockets. "Oh, I already do. Come find me, when you're ready, and we'll figure out our next steps."

Gavan mounted his horse and turned it around. "Can't believe I'm saying this, but it's good to see you again, Tomas. Your kind of chaos might be just what we need here."

24

———————

The afternoon passed quickly. Once General Gavan had ridden away, Tomas had waited for about an hour to make sure the man was well and gone and that no one was watching him. When he was satisfied, he returned to Hardin and the rest of the crew.

After Tomas finished his report, Hardin shook his head. "You're asking us to take a lot on trust."

"It was always going to be that way. But there's nothing illegal about being a host, and Gavan's a man who follows the rules. The way I see it, I'm putting myself in more danger than you are."

Hardin scoffed. "You think you're the only one around here who has a price on his head? Each of us has a warrant out for our arrest."

Tomas hadn't considered that, and wondered if Gavan had. He supposed it was possible that Gavan was going to all this trouble to capture him, but the idea didn't sit right with him. Tomas had risked everything by meeting Gavan alone, and the general hadn't taken advantage of it. "I think we can trust him."

The debate among Hardin's crew was the most vigorous Tomas had yet witnessed from them. Myra and Kyle were strongly against the idea of cooperating with the army. As Tomas listened to Myra, he got the sense she had something personal behind her objections. Perhaps she'd deserted? Kyle just didn't want to take the risk.

Emerson and Tomas both argued the opposite. To Tomas' mind, they didn't have many choices. They needed the army, and there was no way to get that assistance without extending them some trust. He wasn't blind to the risks he was running, but any other plan was even more hopeless. Besides, at the end of the day, he trusted Gavan the same as he trusted Hardin.

In the end, they made a bit of a compromise. They agreed to cooperate, but they wanted to minimize their direct contact with the 34th. Tomas supposed that was reasonable enough, even though it meant he'd have to serve as liaison. They picked up their camp and moved it closer to where the 34th waited for their next maneuver.

Then, while Hardin and the others set up their camp, Tomas went to go find General Gavan. He made no effort to hide, and when he was approached by one of the roving patrol units, he showed them the letter written by the general. Before long, he had an escort walking him through the outskirts of the camp.

Several of the dogs barked at him, which caused sharp looks from his escorts, but Tomas did his best to ignore them. Yes, he was a host, but he pretended that didn't matter. He did notice that his escort grew considerably larger once they realized what he was. But they still let him carry his sword, so it wasn't all bad.

The escort took him directly to the center of the camp, where Tomas encountered a surprising amount of activity.

This close to nightfall, he expected the command area to be quiet. Instead, it was bustling with officers hovering around Gavan like mosquitoes. One of Tomas' escorts peeled off and entered the cloud of officers. It took him a few moments to get Gavan's attention, but once he did, Gavan broke apart from his subordinates and approached Tomas. "Things always do seem to get interesting once you show up, don't they?"

"Sir?"

"Where are the others?"

"Camped about a mile north of here, sir. You have our help, but they wanted to keep a bit of distance."

"Time for you to tell me exactly what kind of help you have, Tomas."

"Four other hosts, sir. Two are expert swords. One archer who's probably the best I've ever seen. And a younger man who's also a strong fighter."

Gavan made a sound in the back of his throat. "I was kind of hoping you had brought more than that."

"Hosts aren't all that easy to come by these days."

"True." Gavan considered for a moment. "About an hour ago, a messenger came to us from Kimson under a white flag. Says that they want to meet, a parley halfway between our camp and the walls, set for tomorrow at dawn."

"You want an escort, sir?"

"Of course I do, but it won't be you, or any host, for that matter. No need to antagonize them until we mean to." Gavan jabbed his thumb back at his officers. "The proposed meeting place is terrible, and we can't decide if we're walking into an ambush or the church just didn't think much about it."

"Move the location," Tomas said. "If you move it closer

to Kimson you can get a better look at its defenses, and their reaction will tell you plenty about their intentions."

"It's not a bad idea. Can you be here tomorrow at dawn? I'll want to talk to you after I get back."

"Yes, sir."

With that, Tomas was dismissed. Gavan returned to the cloud of officers, and Tomas overheard them discussing alternative locations less prone to ambush. Tomas wished there was more he could do, but this wasn't a situation that his presence would improve. He turned around and began the long journey back to Hardin's camp.

He filled the others in on what had happened, and after they speculated for a time, most of them retired for the night.

Tomas was still too worked up to sleep, though, so he watched the stars and the moon overhead. His thoughts wandered, roaming wildly through past, present, and future, never settling on any one subject for more than a few moments. Elzeth stirred, but didn't speak.

In time, Tomas' breathing eased. He lay down right where he was and fell quickly asleep.

The morning came too soon. Elzeth woke him before the sun rose, and he went through his forms with an unusual intensity. There was no one thing he could put his finger on, and yet he felt a growing unease. He supposed there were plenty of things he could point to and blame for his discomfort, but none of them alone explained his feeling.

Not even three repetitions of practicing his forms could fully dispel the sensation.

"Do you feel it, too?" he asked Elzeth.

"What?"

"That unease."

"I feel yours, and I'm still furious about that damned stone, but no."

"I don't like it."

The day was almost too calm. There wasn't enough of a breeze to move the grass. Tomas broke his fast quickly, then said his farewells to Hardin's crew, who was just waking up. Once again, he made the journey to the army camp. As before, Gavan's letter granted him quick access to the camp, and this time his escort was smaller. They took him to the command area, but Gavan and his aides and escort were already gone.

Tomas wanted to follow them. But it was a foolish idea in more ways than he could count. So he settled in to wait.

The next few hours of his life made him wonder if perhaps he was indeed going mad. He kept thinking he was hearing excitement off in the distance, but whenever he looked up, he saw nothing but the orderly operations of the camp. At one point, one of his escorts asked him if something was the matter.

Tomas shook his head and fretted that something in him was broken beyond repair.

"Settle down," Elzeth scolded him. "You're making me want to get up and run around."

"I want to be out there. I want to be involved in that parley."

"Why?"

"In case something goes wrong."

"The most likely way something would go wrong was if you were there. You just want to be there because you always feel like you need to be in the middle of things. If you left things alone sometimes, the world would probably get on just fine."

The words cut deep, largely because they caught him by surprise. "Is that really what you think?"

The sagani's silence was answer enough.

Before Tomas could answer, there was a commotion from the south side of camp, and this wasn't one that Tomas imagined.

He stood up in time to see Gavan and the others riding back. From the looks on their faces, the parley with the church hadn't gone well.

Gavan dismounted and strode toward the command area of the camp. He ordered all his officers to the command tent, but he made a straight line for Tomas.

Tomas stood in place, slightly afraid of what had happened. It crossed his mind that perhaps he'd been betrayed to the church.

But Gavan stopped a few paces in front of him. "Stay here," he said. "This meeting won't take long, and then we have much to discuss."

He turned, but Tomas couldn't let it go without something more. "What happened?"

"They might as well have just declared war," Gavan said.

25

———

Gavan was as good as his word and then some. Tomas had expected at least another hour of waiting. His own days in the army, now long past, had taught him that command meetings were never short affairs. But officers started streaming out of the tent about ten minutes after Gavan went in. Tomas grunted, surprised such a thing was possible.

A few minutes later, Gavan stepped out and gestured for Tomas to join him. One of Tomas' escorts looked profoundly uncomfortable about the idea, but the protest died on her lips when Gavan cut it off.

Tomas hurried in, and Gavan closed the tent flap behind them. Outside, the noises from the rest of the camp increased, and Tomas glanced back at the flap. Gavan waved his concern away. "We're getting ready to march. Nice thing about a dawn parley is that it gives us a full day to react."

"What happened?"

Gavan sat down heavily in a chair and ran a hand through his hair. "They came with demands."

"What?"

Gavan nodded. "Never thought I'd see the day, but here we are. The higher-ups have been debating whether or not this moment has been coming for years. Still, I have to confess I didn't see it coming. One of those things that just doesn't feel real."

Gavan stood back up and went to the map that covered the table in the center of the tent. The topography was well mapped, and figures for units were in their appropriate positions. Gavan ran his finger in a large square that encompassed almost the entire map. "Their claim is that all this land is territory that has been officially ceded to the church, and that we are trespassers. They told us to remove ourselves by dusk, or there would be dire consequences."

"Is it theirs?"

Gavan shrugged. "Who knows? I could see them bribing some lower official in the government to sign them the necessary paperwork. Or hell, even have one of their own do it. We've never cared much about a person's beliefs, but now that the church is growing bolder, we're finding that all of our organizations are riddled with believers. If the Holy Father snaps his fingers, he could cripple no small part of the east. And the legal claiming and assignment of land out here is already a mess. But none of that matters, because I'm here on orders direct from the president."

Tomas listened to the sounds of the camp being packed up. "You leaving?"

"Not a chance. If they want a fight, I'm ready to give them one. If we back down here, it sets a precedent across the country. Kimson isn't even the largest of these new church settlements that was founded in the last year. No, I'm planning on setting up camp just outside their walls. I've got cannons, and if they force my hand, I'll use them on the town."

Tomas swore to himself. "You've got cannons? All the way out here?"

"Six of them, hidden in covered wagons. We've been planning this operation for a while."

Tomas whistled softly. Six cannons would destroy most of the town in short order. He'd been on both sides of the monstrosities, and they were still the most terrifying weapons humans had invented. Memories from long ago, on battlefields far to the east, caused bile to rise in his throat. The unease he'd been feeling thickened, until he felt as though he might throw up. "What's your plan here? What are you trying to accomplish?"

"My written orders? To investigate Kimson and to ensure that no laws are being broken. More specifically, I'm searching for any evidence of a new weapon. My soldiers need to search that town from top to bottom if the church hopes for a peaceful resolution."

"And your unwritten orders?"

"To show the church the president is done bowing to them. They aren't loud about what they do, but they keep scratching out new territory. Believers are everywhere, and they run more towns and cities than anyone wants to admit. Kimson is our chance to push back."

"If they're demanding that you leave, they might have the weapon in there ready to go."

"In which case, we need to take it. But I don't think they have the weapon yet. I get the sense that the cardinal in charge of the settlement believes we won't push too hard. After years of bending to their requests, it's hard to blame him. He thinks we're only here for show."

"What do you want from me?"

"I'm worried about these knights you told me about. A knight is already a problem enough, and they brought a few to the parley, so I know they have at least two squads inside. But if any of them are hosts, things could get bloody really fast if we have to force our way in. I was hoping that you and yours might be willing to stay close by. If there are hosts inside, I'd want you to fight them."

"If you have that many cannons, why take the risk? Level the town and have it done with."

Gavan's stare turned hard. "We need to avoid a repeat of your mistake at Chesterton. If word ever got out that the army had flattened an entire church settlement, it would be hard not to imagine having civil war on our hands. And that must be avoided at all costs. We're still recovering from the last war. Even if they attack first, we need to restrain our responses."

Tomas nodded, understanding even if he didn't completely agree. A large-scale war against the church, against people who were more than willing to become martyrs for their beliefs, was a terrifying prospect. "We'll help in whatever ways we can."

"Thank you. Take those on your way out, so that no one attacks you." Gavan pointed toward half a dozen strips of green fabric. The same color as the army uniforms. "Tie them around your arms."

Tomas gave Gavan a short bow, picked up the fabric, and left the tent. Outside, the camp was already mostly down. Soldiers went about their tasks with practiced efficiency, and Tomas admired the order found within the 34th as much as he did within Hardin's group. He took his leave and returned to Hardin's camp.

Less than an hour later, they were packed up and trailing the army toward Kimson. The sense of unease in Tomas' stomach had settled a bit, which was a welcome change from earlier in the day. Hardin fell into step beside him. "What do you think of General Gavan?"

"He's a competent commander, and decent enough. I think I would have enjoyed serving under him, back in the day."

"The sort of man we can trust?"

"I think so, so long as we don't abuse what rights he gives us. He's pragmatic, but also loyal to the president and his mission. If he thinks we're turning on him, I don't think he'll hesitate to turn those cannons on us."

Hardin gestured toward the army ahead of them. "Never thought I'd be marching with an army again. Mostly expected that if I saw one in more than passing, it would be them besieging Alliston. You got a plan for this cooperation?"

"Not really. Support the 34th as best I can. Make sure the church doesn't have a weapon, and see if we can get into Kimson to see what they're building there."

"Don't like not having something more specific, but that's about all I've come up with, too. Right now my biggest question is how close to set up camp."

"Might as well see if they'll let us camp on the outskirts," Tomas said. "If something happens we'll want to respond quickly, and I'd rather not be running a couple of miles every time we need to pass a message back and forth."

Hardin floated the idea past the others. Myra and Kyle looked like the idea gave them indigestion, but they admitted it didn't make much sense for them to be so far separated. So when the army finally came to a stop, the walls of Kimson well within view, they worked with one of Gavan's officers to find a place to settle. They ended up on the north edge of the camp, about as far away from Kimson as it was possible for them to be. The officer rearranged the patrols so the dogs never came too close to their section of the camp, and Tomas was grateful for the small kindness.

Tomas took out his looking glass and ran it along the wall. He was impressed, and a little surprised, to see how many guards were on top of it. Given the number of buildings he'd seen from the south side of the town, either almost everyone in Kimson served as a guard or there was at least one bunkhouse. Otherwise the numbers didn't make much sense.

He chuckled when he saw a group on the wall with looking glasses making a study of the 34th. For a moment, he thought he caught one of them staring at him just as he studied them. He would have given up most of the money in his pack to know what they were thinking on those walls. The 34th wasn't a large army, but it was still hundreds of soldiers. The cannons remained hidden in wagons for the moment, but even Tomas, in his days with the unnamed units, would have reconsidered picking a fight with a whole army. Were they panicking on the other side of the wall, or were they so confident in their faith, their weapons, and their place in the world that it didn't even occur to them to be afraid?

Tomas eventually stowed his looking glass. The wall was a wall, and it blocked most of the view of the settlement behind it. It was well protected, but he was with an army. He decided to make himself comfortable.

Before he could, a pair of dogs barked loudly behind him. He turned to see a guard patrol pulling at the leashes of their animals. Many of them were trained to attack a host when they smelled one, and these dogs were straining at their leashes. The soldiers who had the misfortune of being attached to the other end fought valiantly, but it looked like it would be a few minutes before they won. The patrol's commanding officer apologized profusely, claiming he had forgotten their routes had changed.

Myra and Kyle stood side by side, as though ready to fight the patrol off. But Hardin waved to the commander, thanked him for the apology, and stood between Myra, Kyle and the dogs. Thanks to him, the situation was quickly defused, and Tomas was once again grateful for the veteran's leadership. Whatever Myra and Kyle had been through, camping so close to the 34th was taking a toll on them.

Afternoon faded into evening, and there was little for them to do except sit around and wait. For once, Tomas found that he didn't mind. Emerson had started a small fire and was preparing the first full meal Tomas had eaten in days. No soldiers of the 34th came to join them, but Tomas didn't sense any hostility from passing soldiers, either.

When they ate supper together, it felt a bit to Tomas like he had finally come home. The army and the people in his small circle might be different, but it was an evening much like any he had experienced with the unnamed units. Hardin and his crew were a part of the army and yet separate, just as they had been back then.

They were halfway through their meal when a messenger came to Hardin. "Orders from the general, sir. He wants you to keep watch tonight. The church issued another ultimatum. Either we leave before sundown, or tonight they attack."

Hardin glanced at the messenger. "What's our plan?"

"The general believes they're bluffing, but he wants the army ready for quick action tonight, including all of you. Everyone's getting a shorter night of rest tonight, sir."

Hardin thanked the messenger, who returned to his duties. Then he turned to the others. "Well, eat up. Looks like we might be in for an exciting night."

26

The fire crackled as Emerson used a long stick to shift the burning logs around. Night had fallen a few hours ago, but the time of greatest darkness had passed as Tolkin rose in the sky. Hardin hadn't ordered anyone to stay up, but they all had anyway. Tomas suspected they all felt some of the same unease that had never quite stopped haunting him. He couldn't explain it, but he'd been a part of enough battles to trust it.

Something was coming.

They swapped stories to pass the time, and now the fire burned low. Tomas split his attention between the group, the settlement in the distance, and his saddlebags. He'd left his pack far enough away from the rest of the group so as not to cause any problems.

Kimson's walls stood quiet watch over the intruding army, but Tomas saw nothing through his looking glass that concerned him. A few lone sentries patrolled the walls. They all carried rifles, but against the advance of the 34th, they would be nothing more than a temporary annoyance.

Across the fire from Tomas, Hardin spun a cup slowly in his hands, a distant look in his eyes. Tomas wanted to know what the man thought so deeply about, but the others took his ponderous silence in stride. Emerson talked animatedly about his new niece, born in a frontier town about a week's ride east of Alliston. Not long before Tomas had arrived, Emerson had been visiting. His extended family didn't know he'd become a host, and had welcomed his company with open arms.

"They even invited me to stay on with them for a time, if I ever felt the urge," Emerson said. "Considering it, once this is done."

"I think you should," Kyle said. "I would, if I had any family that welcomed me."

Emerson nodded. To Tomas, it looked like the young fighter didn't need much convincing.

Myra was the voice of reason. "It's a mighty risk, Emerson. Visiting for a day or two is simple enough, but it's not always easy to hide in plain sight. You know that as well as anyone. All it takes is one small slip and people start to question. These days, it seems like everyone's on the lookout for hosts." She glanced pointedly at Tomas before returning to Emerson. "You get comfortable there, and that slip becomes much more likely. I know you're not asking my opinion, but it seems to me you'd be better served only visiting a day or two at a time. Easier to stay focused."

Emerson stared down at his cup. "Suppose you got a point. Stinks, though. She's a cute girl, and I'd like to be a part of her life."

"Not saying you can't," Myra said. "Just want you to think it through. It's not the way it should be, but sometimes being around less means you'll be closer to her in the end."

Emerson nodded, but looked eager to change the subject. "What about you, Tomas?" he asked. "You have any family?"

"Not that I know of," Tomas said. "I grew up in the sword schools and never really knew anyone related to me by blood. I couldn't say one way or the other."

Tomas glanced at Myra, curious about her family. She answered his unspoken question. "I've got a brother back east. Some important banker who won't even acknowledge that I'm still alive." Myra dismissed Tomas' half-formed sympathy with a casual wave. "It's old news. But I've also got a husband in Alliston. We've been debating whether we should try for a child."

"Really?" Tomas hid his surprise poorly.

Myra laughed. "You don't think I'd make a good mother?"

"Not that at all. It's just that I've only ever seen you as a warrior and as a sword instructor. Easy to forget, sometimes, that there's more to life than all of that." Tomas' own thoughts wandered back to Razin. Would she be on patrol now, keeping the streets safe? He liked to think that she was. The thought opened up a longing that had been scabbed over for weeks. He wasn't sure it would ever heal completely. He wasn't sure he wanted it to. "Do you think you two will try?"

Myra nodded. "I think so. I haven't been a host for too many years, so I'm hopeful I've got quite a bit of time left. Husband's not a host, so he'll be around. Hardin and I both agree I shouldn't go on too many more of these kinds of missions, and that I should focus on training the next generation of Alliston's swords. If this works out and we're forced to take that year off from raiding, it might be the best opportunity I've had." She paused, then looked down at her feet. "Might ask if I can learn whatever secrets to longevity you have, though. If we're going to have a child, I want to be around for as long as possible. Any thoughts you had would be appreciated."

Tomas was delighted to help, and was about to say as much when he thought he heard something. The sound only lasted for a moment, then was gone. He frowned and looked around. It had sounded almost like something whining. Maybe a dog had gotten too close and been upset its master had pulled it away from the hosts? He strained his ears, and Elzeth flickered to life, sharpening his hearing. But all he heard were the murmurs of dozens of campfire discussions, just like this one. He glanced around the fire. "Did any of you hear anything, just now?"

His question was met with blank looks and shaking heads. Tomas tried to convince himself to relax, but the tension between his shoulders wouldn't go away.

"Did you hear it?" Tomas asked Elzeth.

"Thought so, but it was only for a moment."

Instinct demanded that he rise, so he did, attracting every eye around the campfire. Before they could ask, the sound came again.

It was louder and longer this time, a full two seconds at least. It sounded like the high-pitched squeal of metal. Tomas had never heard anything quite like it. It wasn't any sound that could be found in the natural world. The closest noise he could compare it to was that of a train squealing to a stop at a station, but even that didn't do it justice.

The sound was strange enough, but it was made worse by the fact that it came from everywhere all at once. Tomas turned his head, trying to find the source of the sound, but no matter what way he cocked his head, he couldn't even guess.

As suddenly as it had started, it was over.

"Y'all heard *that* though, right?" Tomas asked.

Their wide eyes and darting glances were answer enough. Kyle clutched at his stomach as though he were sick. The disturbance even jarred Hardin out of his reverie. The giant man looked up. "What was that?"

"Trying to figure that out," Myra said. She gestured toward the rest of the army encampment. Tomas needed a moment to see what she wanted him to notice. Hardin's hosts were the only people on their feet. The rest of the camp was getting ready for bed, and several soldiers were preparing for their turn at the watch. Tomas couldn't see a sign of distress or concern anywhere among the soldiers. A few of the closer soldiers shot them worried looks, but that was all.

Tomas looked around, but there was no enemy to be found. The walls of Kimson, at a glance, appeared as quiet as ever. If not for the other hosts, Tomas might have thought he was finally going mad.

"We should—" Tomas never got to finish his idea.

The sound struck again, with no more warning than either of the times before. It vibrated inside of Tomas' skull, coming from everywhere and nowhere all at once. Kyle fell over and vomited, and the other hosts fell to their knees. Myra covered up her ears as Hardin reached for his sword. Tomas stayed on his feet, though his knees felt as though they were ready to buckle.

His eyes sought an attacker, but there was nothing. His new friends rolled in the dirt, Emerson coming close to crashing right into the coals of their campfire.

Beyond their small circle, though, Tomas saw nothing

amiss. The hosts' commotion had attracted attention, and soldiers were standing up and approaching to see if they could help. Whatever was happening, the soldiers were unaffected.

Then Tomas' world went white as a flash, brighter than any bolt of lightning, filled the night sky.

The flash only lasted for a second or two, but it filled the sky and blinded Tomas. It was pure white, tinged with blue. He could discern no origin, nor any destination. Then it was gone, leaving ghostly afterimages wherever he looked.

A moment later, the ground shook hard enough that Tomas almost lost his balance. Far to the east, near the other end of the camp, dirt and grass were blasted into the air as though Gavan had been foolish enough to set up his camp on a bed of lit dynamite. Shredded canvas floated down to the ground as a cloud of dust rose in the dark sky.

The destruction was no symptom of madness. The soldiers might not have heard the squealing sounds, but the attack on their camp was all too real. Soldiers shouted and pointed, and the officers who were still awake barked out orders.

Tomas considered the 34th's reaction to the attack a testament to Gavan's leadership. Less than a minute ago, they had been the far superior force camped outside a settlement that had no chance of resisting their demands.

Now they were under an attack unlike anything they'd ever seen. But neither soldier nor officer fell into panic at the rapid and unexpected change of events. Soldiers worked with their units and focused on the dual tasks of securing their perimeter and aiding those who had been wounded.

Tomas turned his attention from the wider scene to the one directly surrounding him. Of the five hosts, he was the only one standing. The only one who looked like they would be standing anytime soon. Kyle and Hardin were unconscious, but their breathing appeared steady. Myra and Emerson were awake, but they didn't look pleased by that fact. Both were curled into the fetal position, groaning and twisting on the ground.

Tomas knelt next to them, but couldn't see anything obviously wrong with either of them. "Is there anything I can do?" he asked.

"We're good," Myra said through gritted teeth. "But my sagani feels like it's running laps inside my stomach."

"Any ideas?" Tomas asked Elzeth.

"Near as I can tell, they're fine," Elzeth said. "I don't have any better idea what's happening to them than you do."

"Why didn't it hit us so hard?"

"Don't have the slightest."

"Hmm." Tomas stood up and looked around. He thought he saw activity to the south, toward Kimson. In his immediate vicinity, the situation remained unchanged, and there was nothing he could do to help his friends. He squatted down next to Myra. "I'm going to see what else happened. I'll be back soon."

"Go," she said.

Tomas stood and planned his best course of action. The explosion had been to the east, and any danger would be from Kimson to the south. He decided to split the difference and head southeast. He kept his pace to a brisk walk. The green armband across his bicep deterred any suspicious glances, but he could tell that the camp was emptying quickly. The 34th prepared for battle.

Tomas weaved through the tents, one eye always on Kimson. Unfortunately, fires had caught in the camp, destroying tents and filling the air with light and smoke. It made observing the walls difficult. He passed by two covered wagons that rested heavily on their axles. Both were surrounded by squads of infantry, and Tomas hurried to get around them. He caught a glimpse of dark metal within, and the sight alone was enough to cause him to falter and miss a step.

He recovered and hurried on, putting the monstrous cannons behind him. Hopefully they wouldn't fire tonight.

He reached the site of the destruction a minute later. Whatever power had caused this was beyond that of dynamite, beyond even that of cannons. Tomas stopped and looked down. He stood on prairie ground, the same as countless miles he'd walked before. The grass was trampled underfoot thanks to the presence of the army, but it was otherwise unremarkable.

A few steps in front of his feet, though, there was a sharp line in the ground, a demarcation. The ground itself had been blasted away, maybe six to eight inches deep. Dark clay was underneath, and the air here was still thick with fine dirt. Moans of the wounded and dying filled Tomas' ears, as well as the orders given by the soldiers fighting to save their friends.

The destruction wasn't absolute. Patches of grass could still be found. Tomas wrapped a bandanna around his face to keep the dirt out of his mouth and nose, then forged ahead. What kind of weapon did something like this?

He uncovered part of the answer when he found the first body. Its limbs were frozen at odd angles, and there was no doubt the woman was dead. But there was no sign of external injury. Tomas saw only a little blood, and there were none of the cuts from shrapnel he would have expected from a cannon shell. So it wasn't any explosion Tomas was familiar with.

The destruction continued for at least a hundred paces, though it was difficult for Tomas to tell for sure. Dust obscured his vision.

Behind him, a commotion erupted. Tomas spun around and cursed his poor visibility. He hurried west, seeking a place with a better view.

Instead, a stiff breeze suddenly rose, clearing much of the dust. It gave Tomas his first clear view of Kimson's walls in minutes. The walls were no longer empty. From one side of the northern wall to the other, guards stood nearly side by side, and they were all carrying rifles. Tomas swore, unable to calculate the cost of Kimson's defense. He'd never seen so many rifles in one place.

Fortunately, Gavan hadn't been foolish enough to set up his camp within effective rifle range. But the guards on the wall drew the camp's attention. Off to the west, Tomas saw Gavan himself, ordering the army into formation.

Despite the surprise, the 34th ordered itself quickly. Within minutes soldiers were lined up and awaiting their next command. Tomas kept himself out of the way, content to watch this battle unfold for now. How would Gavan respond to the attack?

The answer came soon enough, as Tomas watched the slow movement of six heavy wagons, each pulled by a team of horses. The wagons were placed and the coverings came off, revealing the mounted cannons. Soldiers scurried around them, making them ready to fire.

In Kimson, the guards continued to stand on the wall without any apparent fear.

Tomas was rooted in place, watching the standoff between the two forces. Gavan had the cannons, but no knowledge of what waited behind the walls. And he knew that whatever happened here would have repercussions across the nation. Tomas felt the same tension in his body. He wanted nothing more than to run forward and charge the walls of Kimson, but he kept his position.

One minute passed, followed by another. Soldiers fidgeted, their hands running to swords, bows, and rifles. The cannons stood, silent and impassive. No order was given.

Then Tomas heard the same squealing noise he'd heard before. It was loud and clear, coming from everywhere and nowhere. But it only lasted for a moment. He braced himself, ready for another attack from that horrible weapon.

Instead, the guards on Kimson's walls started to leave their posts. There was no fear in their actions. They weren't retreating. To Tomas' eye, it looked more like they were finishing up with their watch duty, like they'd never expected to fire their rifles at all.

He frowned, the unease that had been his constant companion for the past day suddenly knotting tighter. This had all been planned, and those squealing noises that only hosts could hear had something to do with it.

When Gavan didn't immediately launch his attack in response, Tomas guessed the rest of the night would be relatively quiet. The standoff was decided, at least for now.

He turned back toward where the hosts were camped, eager to check on his new friends.

Tomas hurried in their direction. It didn't take long, as the whole army camp was in formation to the south. When he caught his first glimpse of the hosts' campsite, he broke out into a run.

Their space was in ruins, and the only host who remained was Myra, who lay very still in the dirt, surrounded by blood.

28

Tomas ran to Myra and fell beside her. She was curled on her side, arms wrapped tight around her stomach. He saw her chest rise a fraction of an inch, and his own heart skipped a beat. Blood poured from between her hands, though, a constant stream that didn't bode well.

He turned her onto her back. She fought for a moment, but had no strength to resist. She flopped onto her back and her arms lost their grip on her stomach. Tomas saw the full wound for the first time, and it was worse than he imagined. She'd been cut open almost from side to side. The cut was deep enough that Tomas could see her organs within, along with more blood than one person could afford to lose.

Myra was alive, but her continued survival was a question Tomas didn't have the answer to. If her sagani had any sense, it would be healing the internal injuries first. To give her the best fighting chance, then, he needed to stop as much of the bleeding as he could. Right now her sagani was fighting a losing battle.

He ran to where he had stashed his pack, breathing a quick sigh of relief when he saw that it hadn't been disturbed. He flung open the pack, then couldn't help but notice the soft blue glow from the shard of the nexus. It was an option, but one he discarded quickly. The last time he'd tried to heal someone with a nexus, it had killed them. If he was certain that Myra was going to die, he'd try it. At the very least, it would save the sagani within. But not unless there was no other choice.

Instead, he grabbed a roll of bandages from the pack, then rushed back to where Myra lay. He unwrapped the bandages and took one look at the instructor. "Sorry, but this is going to hurt a lot." She was too involved in her own struggles to hear him.

He squeezed the sides of her cut together. Her eyes went wide with pain as she cursed, but Tomas ignored her as he wrapped the bandage tightly around her waist. He chose speed over gentleness, earning him a heaping serving of curses. Soon it was done. Her breath came in deep, shuddering gasps, but he had her wound wrapped up tightly. He looked her up and down for other injuries. She had a cut across her right wrist, which he also quickly bandaged up. Fortunately, it had missed the artery there.

Then there was nothing left for him to do. The rest of her healing was in her sagani's hands. He kept a close watch over her. If it looked like her sagani couldn't heal her quickly enough, he'd put the shard in her hand and hope for the best.

He noticed a lot of activity to the south, from the main part of the camp, but he ignored it. For now, this was the one thing he could do, and his focus remained fixed. Only one other thought dominated his attention, and that was that all this had been orchestrated. Once again, he'd underestimated the church.

Tolkin was near to setting by the time he rose from his

vigil. The worst threat to her life had passed. Myra's breathing was now slow and steady, and the bleeding had slowed. She'd fallen into a slumber that Tomas knew from experience she wouldn't wake from anytime soon. But when she did, she'd be hungry.

Confident that she wouldn't die if he left her side, Tomas stood and stretched. He already had a good idea of what had happened to the others, but it was worth confirming.

There had been a fight at the camp. That much, at least, was plenty obvious. Thankfully, it made Tomas' life easier because blood had been spilled. He wasn't sure he'd be able to follow tracks across a prairie that was already filled with them, especially at night. He followed the blood. It traced a path that went north for a while, then wheeled around sharply to the west. He passed over a rise to a small draw that ran north to south. There, the tracks turned south, and Tomas followed them. They ended near the shore of the lake.

He'd held onto some small hope that he'd catch up to them, but the group had moved quickly, even carrying Hardin's bulk. There wasn't much about the attack Tomas could say for certain, but he could make plenty of guesses without a problem. He took one last look around, then retraced his steps back to their camp.

Myra was still there, and some of the color had returned to her skin. Tomas made sure she was comfortable, then walked deeper into the camp. Soldiers had returned to their campfires, but it didn't look like anyone would be sleeping soon. Tomorrow would be a long day.

The command area was a study in controlled chaos. Officers came and went in a constant stream, bearing either orders or information. Tomas prepared to make himself comfortable and wait, but there was no need. The moment he was spotted by the general's honor guard, he was whisked into the command tent.

Gavan looked up, his look sharp enough to cut stone. This was a side of the general Tomas hadn't seen, and he tread cautiously. "Sir?"

"I've been looking for you."

"Sorry, sir. But I think that Hardin and the other hosts were the primary objective of this attack," Tomas said.

The tent went quiet at the claim. Tomas knew how it must sound, especially to the officers gathered here who had lost soldiers, but he believed it to be true. A few of the officers looked like they wanted to lay hands on Tomas, but they had the discipline to restrain themselves. Gavan, unfortunately, didn't look any happier. "You're telling me that Kimson unleashed whatever the hell that weapon was, killed almost a hundred of the nation's finest soldiers, and then packed their walls with guards, just to attack you?"

"Not attack, sir. Kidnap."

The command tent turned positively icy. "Explain yourself," Gavan demanded.

"Just prior to the attack, we heard an unusual sound, sir. One that I don't believe any of your soldiers heard. I believe that it was a signal, sent from one host outside the walls to one inside. The attack was triggered, which disabled most of our unit. In the confusion following the attack from the mysterious weapon, our camp was raided and three of the hosts taken away. The fourth was left for dead. Then another signal was given, which told the guards to abandon the walls and deescalate tensions."

"And why are you here, telling me all this? You don't have a scratch on you."

"No, sir. For an unknown reason, the weapon didn't

affect me the way it did the others. I was on the west side of the camp, looking for ways to help after the attack."

"Can you prove any of this?"

"No, sir. But the hosts are gone. They've been taken back to Kimson via the lake. I tracked them that far. I believe that if our capture wasn't *the* primary reason for the attack, it was at least one of several."

Gavan digested the information slowly. "Any speculation as to why the church would kidnap the hosts?"

"No, sir. But the weapon that caused the destruction has something to do with our powers. We heard it before the attack. Did any of you see the flash before?"

The blank looks on the faces of the other officers said more than enough. Tomas pushed forward before they could ask him too many questions he didn't know the answer to. "Whatever that weapon is, it has something to do with either hosts or sagani. That's as much as I can guess."

Gavan nodded. "Thanks for the report. We'll take it under advisement as we decide our next steps."

"Sir." Tomas bowed, knowing full well when he wasn't wanted.

Before he could leave, though, a messenger came in with a letter. He handed it to Gavan. "Word from Kimson, sir. They want to meet at dawn to discuss the terms of your surrender."

29

———

Tomas was keeping watch over Myra when a package arrived for him, delivered by a nervous messenger. The sun hadn't quite risen yet. Despite being up all night, Tomas felt no exhaustion. He worried about his friends being held in Kimson, and swore all sorts of vengeance if they were harmed.

He'd been promptly ejected from the command tent after the ultimatum had been given, but Tomas didn't mind. The facts of the matter remained unchanged. He couldn't get into Kimson on his own. He was reliant on the army, and what the 34th decided wasn't up to him. There was nothing to be done except wait and follow the currents in whichever way they pulled him.

The package came as a surprise. Tomas opened it and frowned at what he found within. He looked up at the messenger, who handed him a letter. It had been penned quickly by Gavan.

Orders.

"Any questions?" the messenger asked.

Tomas shook his head. They were straightforward enough. The messenger departed, hurrying away a lot faster than he'd approached. Tomas watched him leave, then turned to Myra. "Looks like I'll be off again. Gavan says they'll keep watch over you, but I'll be back as soon as I can. With any luck, I'll soon return with our friends, too."

He didn't know if she heard him, but it made him feel better to tell her his plans.

He changed into the army uniform quickly. The color made him frown. Once, it had represented everything he had stood against. He would have given his life to cover it in the blood of his enemies. Now it hardly seemed important at all, and he wondered what that said about the man he had been. Or perhaps what it said about the man he was now. He pushed the thoughts aside as he threw the uniform on, impressed by how well it fit. Someone in the command tent had a sharp eye for his size.

Then he returned to the command area. He introduced himself to the captain of Gavan's honor guard, who looked as pleased to have him joining them as he would to suffer a broken nose. The captain only had one additional order that hadn't been found in Gavan's letter. "If you see a dog, peel off and join the column somewhere farther behind. We don't want them knowing a host is with us, especially one as well known as you. Is that clear?"

"Yes, sir."

He loitered in the area while the general prepared to leave. It didn't take long. By the time the sun broke over the horizon, Gavan and his honor guard marched toward the walls of Kimson under a white flag.

The church hadn't even bothered to set up a tent. A tall man, wearing the robes of a cardinal, stood in the center of the road, flanked by two lone knights. The protection seemed meager, but they were well within rifle range, and Tomas noted a lot of rifles on the wall. The sight gave him a powerful urge to be anywhere but where he was.

But dressed as he was, there was nothing that made him stand out among Gavan's much larger retinue. The cardinal hadn't brought any dogs, so Tomas had little to fear. He was just one face in the crowd.

Gavan made a gesture that brought the rest of the honor guard to a halt, then he joined the cardinal. For a moment, Tomas thought the general might actually be foolish enough to attack. Gavan stood stiffly, as though it took all his control not to draw his sword.

Which, Tomas supposed, probably wasn't all that far from the truth.

The cardinal, by contrast, was the very image of grace and polite civility. One would be forgiven for thinking he was the host of some social function back east. "General Gavan, thank you for coming to our summons." His voice was higher-pitched than Tomas had expected, possessing an almost musical cadence. But every word was designed to cut.

"What do you want?" Gavan asked.

"For you and your army to turn around and leave Kimson in peace. This is not a place of war, and you remain trespassers, despite my warning yesterday."

"And you murdered eighty-seven of the nation's finest soldiers last night, with a weapon you have no right to possess."

The cardinal's face betrayed nothing. He studied Gavan for a moment. "Did you know that before I joined the church, I was an artist?"

Gavan shook his head, clearly confused by the change in topic.

The cardinal wasn't deterred. "I learned many valuable lessons in those days, but perhaps one of the most important was the role of perspective. You're familiar with perspective, aren't you, general?"

"Of course." Gavan looked closer to drawing his sword than ever before.

"When I was studying my art, I learned how important it is to get perspective right. All it takes is a small mistake and nothing in your drawing or painting looks real. A slight change in perspective makes the whole world look different. To make it look false."

"What's your point?"

"I understand your perspective, General Gavan. You have faithfully served your government for decades, and because of that, you see your government as the source of all good. As a keeper of order. But as a cardinal, and as a believer, I see the world from a slightly different angle. A truer angle."

Gavan took half a step forward, as though he intended to draw. The knights shifted in response, and Gavan forced himself to stillness. The cardinal continued his monologue as though nothing had happened. "In the church, we see the world as it truly is, and this land you think is your own is nothing of the sort. This land is ours, and we will defend it from you as though you were a foreign invader."

The cardinal cut off Gavan's reply with a quick gesture. "There is nothing to negotiate. There is nothing to argue. I gave you a chance yesterday to retreat, but you chose to spit in my face by moving your army closer. I take no offense, though. Belief can be hard for some to embrace. But now you have seen our resolve. Thankfully, for your sakes, we are merciful. If you leave here by noon today, we shall let you leave in peace. But if we see so much as a hint of aggression, you can rest assured we will not hesitate to destroy you all. Now, be gone from here, and have a nice day, general."

30

Gavan burst into his command tent like a raging bull, pacing back and forth as his officers piled in behind him. The captain of his honor guard pushed Tomas in, too. The host found a space near the corner of the tent where he could observe everything but remain out of the way.

Gavan mastered his rage with a visible effort. "Opinions, now."

"They've as much as declared war," one officer said.

"If we retreat here, they're going to claim independence for all of their new settlements," another added.

"But what can we do? We don't know a thing about the weapon that attacked us last night," a third chimed in.

The comments came in fast, but always one at a time. The officers had the restraint not to speak over one another. The discussion took shape quickly. The 34th found itself between a rock and a hard place. If they attacked with the cannons, they risked turning the town into martyrs. They didn't know if they would be successful, either. The weapon hung over their decision like a boulder held above their heads with a fraying rope.

But retreating wasn't any more palatable. That decision gave the church everything it wanted, and they left with nothing gained. Tomas saw how the idea of their soldiers dying without recompense weighed on the officers' minds. The only time the conversation grew heated was when it referenced those who had already died.

It didn't take long for the arguments to reach their conclusion, and Gavan ordered silence once the officers started repeating points that had already been made.

At the end of the day, the decision was Gavan's alone, and Tomas sympathized with the man. There were choices that almost certainly changed the course of history, and this felt like one.

From where Tomas watched in the corner, the scene might as well have been a painting. Gavan stood, separate from the groupings of the lesser officers. He had both his hands on the table in the center of the room, and he stared at the map as though there were answers hidden somewhere upon it. Officers stood around the room, straight-backed and staring at their commander, waiting for their orders. Behind them, the flap of the tent caught the morning breeze. The air felt thick, and it was difficult to draw a full breath. The silence had a weight, and it rested squarely on Gavan's shoulders.

The general let out a long, slow sigh. "Very well, then. War it is."

~

Tomas returned to Hardin's camp. There, he found Myra sitting and eating while a couple of enlisted soldiers maintained a defensive perimeter. They let Tomas through without question and he sat down next to Myra. "It's good to see you up," he said.

"Doesn't feel too good, though."

"I'd imagine not. I'm a bit surprised to see you moving, honestly."

"You and me both. I thought I was dead for sure. I hear I have you to thank for the bandages."

Tomas waved her gratitude away. "I meant that I'm surprised you're awake. That injury should have taken at least a day to heal this far. At least in my experience with similar wounds."

Myra shrugged. "Don't really know how bad it was, but if I healed faster, I'd place the blame squarely on that damned shard. It's got my insides all twisted up and it feels like my sagani is trying to run from one end of the country to the other inside my stomach. Not to mention that all I can think about is rummaging through your pack and grabbing it."

"Sorry. I didn't even think about that." He'd left his pack closer to the center of Hardin's camp after healing Myra. Too many other concerns had been fighting for his attention, and he'd not even bothered to move it away. "I'm glad you didn't give in."

"Hardin warned me plenty about the nexus."

She'd been lucky that when she woke up she was cognizant enough to exert the control, but Tomas let the matter go. He'd made a mistake, but fortunately it hadn't cost them anything. Perhaps it had even helped. Now he had an ally, right when he most needed one. "I can guess a lot of it, but what happened?"

Myra grimaced and sat up straighter. "They hit us just after you left. Emerson and I were starting to recover, but we were still in a lot of pain. More than a full squad of knights. Emerson and I tried to fight, but weren't in any condition.

One knocked him out cold, and they left me for dead. I didn't even scratch them."

"Hosts?" Tomas had seen how well Myra fought.

"Don't think so," she said. "Tough to trust my perception from the time, but I think they were just knights."

That made sense, if Tomas thought about it for a moment. The church had to have known the effect the weapon had on hosts, so they wouldn't have sent any.

"Anyway, they bound Hardin, Emerson, and Kyle and took them away. Back north, as far as I could see," Myra finished.

"I tracked them to Kimson," Tomas said.

"Figured. Seems like things have been busy, though. What's been happening here?"

Tomas filled her in quickly, ending with the most recent events. "Gavan plans on attacking the settlement, and soon."

Myra took the news with surprising calm. "Our friends are in there."

"Which is why I came. I wanted to let you know that I'm going to try to get them out."

"How?"

"Under the cover of cannon fire."

Myra's eyes went wide as she swore. "You're mad."

"It's been said before, and I don't like the idea any more than you do. But Gavan assures me his crews are well trained. He blasts down the walls, then we run in and rescue our friends while they fight for control of the settlement."

Myra laughed out loud. "You make it sound so easy. Like there aren't knights, knights that are hosts, dozens of rifles, and some mysterious super-weapon that disables hosts behind those walls."

"Well, see, you make it sound too hard." He kept his tone light, but even he couldn't deny his terror at what was about to happen. He expected it would be worse than the battles he'd fought during the war, and he did his very best to forget as much about those as he could. "But we need to know what the church has in there, and I won't leave without trying to save them."

Myra leaned her head back against her pack. She closed her eyes. "I don't want to do it," she confessed.

"Then don't. I didn't even think you were going to be awake yet. I came here hoping to get you up and get you running away before the battle started."

Tears trickled down the sides of her face. "I really didn't think this would be the way it ended, you know? Once I found Hardin and Alliston, I really believed it would be madness that got me."

Tomas knelt down next to her. "You'll find no judgment here, Myra. There's no need for you to follow me in there."

Myra snorted. "I've seen the way you fight. If you don't have me watching your back you'll be dead before you even reach the wall."

"I'm serious, Myra. There's nothing wrong with turning around and starting a family, just like you said."

She shook her head. "Sounds nice, but I wouldn't be able to live with myself."

Tomas didn't know what else to say. He'd respect her decision either way, but she was right. His chances of surviving were much higher with her around. To the south, he could feel the atmosphere of the camp changing. To prevent an attack from the weapon, Gavan's officers were spreading the word quietly among the troops. There would be no formations this morning. The cannons would fire, and that would be the signal for the charge to begin.

When it happened, Tomas needed to be near the front.

Unfortunately, he couldn't give her the time she wanted

to make her decision. He extended his hand. "On the bright side, you'll get my company as part of the deal."

She took his hand and he pulled her up. "Not too late to reconsider, is it?"

They took a few minutes to gather their supplies. Tomas left his pack behind, but he took the shard in a gloved hand and slipped it into his pocket. Myra saw him do so and gave him a disgruntled look.

"Sorry," Tomas said. "But so long as it's on me, you'll be less interested in trying to grab it, right?"

She laughed out loud, which sounded out of place in the subdued camp. "I suppose that's true enough."

"You good?" He'd been watching her. She moved stiffly, but considering she'd been on the very edge of death less than twelve hours ago, she was looking remarkably healthy.

"Tired, but can't complain. Let's go."

Together, they worked their way through the camp.

In a way, it was like walking through a quiet nightmare. Everywhere they walked, soldiers were preparing to fight while pretending like they weren't. Cookfires were put out and swords were examined. They passed one of the wagons with the mounted cannons, where soldiers appeared to be loitering around.

Wherever Tomas looked, he saw the tension in the soldiers. Noon was just a bit more than an hour away, and if they didn't start packing up soon, the church would suspect the extent of their ruse.

It wouldn't be long now.

They found their way to the front, where the tension among the soldiers was highest. Here, no one spoke, and few even pretended to be going about their daily tasks. Tomas wondered if they were fooling anyone on the wall.

He halfway expected to hear that whine once again that heralded the coming of the weapon.

Tomas and Myra took up a position with the others, sitting on the ground and pretending to relax. Not long after they sat down, an officer came by with a watch in hand. "Four minutes," he said.

There were nods around the circle, and the officer moved on.

"Try to stay close," Tomas said. "We'll find them."

Myra nodded, but did a poor job hiding her growing nervousness. Tomas wasn't sure he was much better. The only other warning they would get was that of the cannons themselves, and Tomas feared that when he heard them, even he would freeze. His palms started to sweat as he imagined the cannonballs flying over his head.

"I will not freeze," he whispered, so quietly so that only he could hear it. "I will not freeze."

He was still repeating the phrase when the whole world seemed to explode around him.

31

Tomas had lost count of the years it had been since he'd heard a cannon go off. It wasn't enough years for his body to forget the mind-rending terror of the weapons, but it had been long enough for him to forget just how loud they were.

Especially when one was almost directly behind them.

The first salvo ripped across the battlefield, one resounding boom followed by the next as the other cannons followed the first. Even though Tomas had expected the blasts, he still jumped halfway out of his pants when they went off.

Had he been alone, he might have frozen in place. The power of the cannons was so great, and Tomas knew all too well what the guards on the walls were about to experience. Even Ghosthands, for all his strength and cunning, didn't terrify Tomas the way cannons did.

But he wasn't alone.

The moment the first cannon went off, the officer in charge of the group Tomas and Myra had joined was on his feet, urging them forward. Tomas joined them, not because he made some heroic choice, but because everyone around him was leaving and he didn't want to be left behind.

The cannons focused their fire on one section of the north wall of Kimson, and the effects were even more disastrous than Tomas remembered. As the smoke cleared, he saw that a whole section of the wall was simply gone. The wooden walls had never been designed to withstand direct cannon fire.

The attack had caught the defenders by surprise, too, as the rifles that remained on the wall were slow to respond. Either that, Tomas figured, or he simply couldn't hear them over the ringing in his ears.

Tomas and the others were within a hundred paces of the walls when the cannons fired again. He flinched despite knowing the cannons would have shifted their aim. Now they sought to tear down other parts of the wall and provide cover from the rifles. Tomas didn't see how well it worked, but neither he nor anyone near him had gotten shot, so he supposed the answer was "good enough."

Then the cannons went silent, which was again according to plan. Gavan's soldiers were too close to the wall, and would soon be inside the settlement. If the fighting went poorly, they would retreat and let the cannons level Kimson, but the weapon inside was worth the risk of lives. They needed to know what the weapon did and how it worked.

At the moment, none of that mattered to Tomas. He charged forward like a bloodhound on a scent. A bullet kicked up dirt less than foot in front of him, but he didn't slow. He leaped through the gaping hole in the wall and stepped foot for the very first time in Kimson.

His first impression of the settlement was that it lacked

any imagination. He couldn't help comparing it to Alliston, or Jonasson, or other settlements that had just been started. Kimson had developed much more in a shorter time, but it had lost something in the haste. In the host settlements, it was clear that most houses had been built following the same basic pattern. But each contained their own individuality, their own personality. Maybe one had more windows, or a larger porch. Some owners carved patterns into door frames. Others added on rooms for larger families.

Stepping into Kimson felt a little like stepping into a maze of mirrors. Every house was the exact same as its neighbor, a startling uniformity that was almost disorienting. His eyes naturally searched for anything unique to latch onto, but every building was the same for as far as he could see.

Thankfully, he had little time to think about it.

Like any visiting dignitary, he was greeted by a contingent of Kimson's finest. Unfortunately, they were armed and had little interest in entertaining guests. Tomas had made it a dozen steps into the city when a group of riflemen marched into the street in front of him. They brought their rifles to bear, aiming down the street toward the open wound in the wall.

Tomas ducked onto a side street just before the first volley fired. Bullets whined through the air where he'd been, and the unfortunate soldiers behind him ran headfirst into the attack. Bodies fell with muted thumps.

Tomas sheathed his sword and launched himself at one of the houses. He got a foot up on a windowsill and leaped off it, grabbing onto the top of the roof and pulling himself up and over with one smooth motion. Then he ran up the roof and down the other side, leaping from one identical house to the next.

His approach hid him from the riflemen in the street, but it exposed him to the rifles on the wall. A few guards had turned to punish the soldiers of the 34th for trespassing, and Tomas' antics drew their attention. Bullets tore up the roof as Tomas climbed the north side, and Tomas slid down the south to break line of sight. He dropped onto the street the riflemen had appeared from, directly to the west of them.

Those at the end of the line turned as he fell, but they were too late. Tomas sprinted forward, drew his sword, and fell upon the unit with a vengeance. Powerful as the rifles were at range, Tomas had the upper hand once he was among them. He carved his way through, then ran for cover as the last man fell. The rifles on the wall, which had remained silent while he was among friends, fired again, chewing up the corner of the house he hid behind.

He'd done enough here. The unit of rifles had hoped to make the hole in the wall a natural chokepoint, but when Tomas risked a glance back at the wall, he saw that the 34th was pouring through like water through a broken dam. They would establish a perimeter that would allow others to follow with less risk.

That was when Tomas realized he didn't know where Myra had gone. She'd been right beside him when he'd come through the wall, but she wasn't anywhere to be found now. He glanced back at the street, afraid she'd been caught by the first volley from the rifles. But he didn't see her body among the fallen.

His second glance told him the 34th had the assault well in hand. What rifles remained on the wall were focused on the soldiers rushing into the settlement.

The 34th didn't need his help. And besides, he wasn't really here for them. He cracked his knuckles and looked around. His friends were here, and if he had to guess, they were somewhere deeper in. He suspected that was where he'd find Myra, too.

Tomas turned his back on the battle and explored deeper into Kimson.

32

———

Tomas poked his head around the corner, breathing a quick sigh of relief when he saw the street ahead was clear. This battle made him feel blind, and he realized just how much he had come to depend on his sharpened hearing on smaller battlefields. How many times had Elzeth saved his life because he'd heard an ambusher or attacker before they could strike?

At the Battle of Kimson, the rifles and cannons shouted too loudly. Tomas could hear little except the reports from the weapons, and his inability to hear his surroundings clearly left him feeling vulnerable, worried there was always an enemy behind him.

Tomas scurried around the corner and ran down the street, eyes darting left, right, and up. He was heading south, toward the lake and the church, whose steeple he could sometimes now see between the rows of identical houses. His direction was nothing but intuition, an educated guess. Everything important in Kimson would be either in the church or near it.

He was running past a house when one of the front

windows exploded outward, showering Tomas with jagged glass as a knight leaped through. The knight tackled Tomas, catching him by surprise. They rolled once and the knight came up on top. He had a dagger in his right hand and he punched down at Tomas' chest. Tomas got his left arm up in time, deflecting the blow in exchange for a deep cut along his forearm.

The knight punched down again, but Tomas dropped his sword to free his hand. He reached for the knight's neck with his right hand as he fought off the dagger with his left. Even with Elzeth burning bright, the fight was close. But Tomas got his hand around the knight's throat. With a roar, he flung the knight to the side.

The knight rolled and was on his feet in a moment, but it was enough time for Tomas to grab his sword and find his own feet. The knight tossed the dagger to his left hand as he drew a thin, long blade with his right. Tomas attacked, but the knight's thin blade flickered close to Tomas' heart and forced him to back up.

The knight pursued, and the tip of his weapon carved red lines across Tomas' chest. It didn't look like much of a weapon, but it was fast and its reach was longer than Tomas' own sword. The knight seemed content to carve him up in bits and pieces.

Lacking that, the knight was waiting for reinforcements.

Either way, Tomas needed a quick response. He raised his sword as though committing to an overhead strike, then he threw his blade.

The knight blocked the throw, but it occupied his attention for the precious second Tomas needed to close the space between them. As Tomas' sword fell to the dirt, Tomas grabbed at the knight's wrist and pulled him to the ground. He twisted the wrist and yanked on the arm, and it broke with a satisfying crack. He finished the knight by driving a foot into his face.

None of the injuries were fatal, but the knight was out of the fight. Tomas grabbed his sword and continued farther into Kimson, wary of more knights lying in wait.

The farther he proceeded into the settlement, the more use his hearing became. Gunfire still echoed behind him, but there were enough houses between him and it that it was no longer deafening. So Tomas heard the sound of steel against steel before he saw the fight. He ran toward it, more than halfway certain what he would find.

As he expected, he found that Myra was the source of the sound. She was engaged with another knight, and the battle was a sight to behold. Tomas had seen plenty of evidence of Myra's skill, but he'd not yet seen her at her best.

The knight was larger and stronger than her, but Myra had the edge in speed. She never let herself get caught in a contest of strength, and she moved like water around the knight's strikes. But her advantage in speed wasn't enough to negate the knight's longer reach, and the man studiously avoided committing too much to a strike. Tomas watched them pass one another twice in as many seconds, but neither could land the fatal cut that would end the fight.

Tomas joined the fray. He cut at the knight, then danced away as the knight countered. It wasn't much of a contribution, but it was enough. The knight wasn't fast enough to fight them both, and Myra cut into the opening provided.

"Thanks," she said as the knight fell. "Sorry we got separated, but I ducked the other way on that first street, then couldn't follow after you. Hoped we'd meet back up deeper in."

"You're also assuming they're somewhere near the church?"

"Absolutely."

"Any other resistance? I killed a knight a ways back, too."

She shook her head. "I think most of the guards are fighting with the 34th. Not sure exactly how the knights have positioned themselves, though. This is the first one I've come across."

Tomas frowned. The sounds of their fight hadn't drawn any other attention, and he didn't hear any shouts of knights finding the body of their other friend. "Feels like we're being delayed."

"Then we should get there faster."

It wasn't much of a plan, but it was exactly what he was thinking. "Let's go."

They ran forward, keeping close to the houses that they passed. It opened them up to ambushes like the one Tomas had encountered, but it kept them safe from any rifles on the wall. Tomas accepted the trade-off gladly.

Their advance was eerily uncontested, though. No guards fired at them, and no knights leaped at them. After just a few minutes they reached the end of the houses.

The difference in the settlement, right after Tomas had gotten used to the rows of identical houses, was jarring. The houses ended at a street that was three times as wide as any other, a street which put Tomas more in mind of a moat than a road.

On the other side of the moat was the church, as well as a group of buildings that looked like they served a variety of purposes. All of which was defended by two lone knights, standing in the middle of the wide street as though they didn't have a care in the world. Myra made to charge, but

Tomas held out a hand to stop her. The hairs on the back of his neck were standing on end.

He studied the scene. The knights didn't seem bothered by the wait. If anything, the matching smirks on their faces only grew wider.

They were definitely being delayed, then. For the weapon?

Tomas didn't see any obvious traps, but he supposed it wouldn't be a very good trap if a quick glance revealed it.

Behind the pair of knights, the church stood tall at the center of an assortment of buildings. One long rectangular structure reminded Tomas of a barracks, and one of the buildings to the east contained a forge. The building that seemed most out of place, though, was a round stone building that made Tomas think of a small, squat arena without a roof.

Past the church, closer to the lake, were the buildings Tomas had seen when he first glimpsed Kimson.

Except for the two knights, nothing moved.

As usual, the only way to answers was to keep pressing forward. He took a deep breath. "Be careful," he said.

Myra snorted.

Together, they advanced on the knights, who waited for them to step into striking distance.

Tomas expected the knights to wait until he and Myra attacked, but he was wrong. The knights launched themselves at the pair as soon as they closed to within a dozen paces. And they were inhumanly fast.

Tomas had suspected, as soon as he'd seen them. Something about the pair had been off.

Elzeth flared brighter, and Tomas met his opponent as Myra met her own.

Within the space of a heartbeat, Tomas had no choice but to retreat.

It wasn't just the knight's skill, which was as impressive as any of the warriors'. It was the fervor and disregard for personal safety. The knight laughed maniacally as he advanced, his sword carving up the space between them without a single thought given to his own life.

Even with Elzeth burning just short of unity, Tomas couldn't track the knight's weapon. His style was either unique or mad, and he couldn't predict it. He stepped back again and again, grateful the street was as wide as it was. They were close enough Tomas felt the heat radiating off the knight. If the knight wasn't careful, he'd burn up his own organs.

Somehow, Tomas didn't think his opponent would care.

Across from him, Myra wasn't faring any better. Her opponent wasn't as careless as Tomas', but his speed and skill more than made up for the difference. Myra wasn't forced to retreat, but she wasn't making an inch of progress.

Tomas waited for an opening, but the assault continued unabated.

The knight couldn't fight like this forever. Eventually, he had to tire. A human body could only endure so much, even as a host.

But the longer the fight went on, the more Tomas doubted his senses. The knight didn't slow. If anything, he cut even faster than before. Tomas swore. He was marching the wrong way, and strongly suspected they didn't have much time left to find their friends.

"Unity?" he asked.

Before Elzeth could respond, Tomas heard the sound he'd been dreading since the night before. Up close, it sounded like dozens of souls screaming in agony, ground against the gears of some giant machine. Tomas' stomach twisted in knots, and he stepped back, barely able to hold onto his sword.

Fortunately, his opponent suffered as much and more. As soon as the sound began, he halted his advance, grimacing against the pain.

Tomas looked around, desperately searching for the source of the sound. But as before, it sounded like it was coming from everywhere at once.

Then the world flashed as lightning filled the cloudless sky, and it was too late.

33

The pain was far worse than before. Tomas collapsed to his knees as his legs turned to jelly. Elzeth screamed, and Tomas screamed with his partner. It felt like a wild animal had torn him open with sharp claws and was rearranging his organs as it searched for the best bits to devour. A wave of power rippled through the air, originating from the open-aired arena. The wave crashed over Tomas.

He immediately regretted being so close to the weapon. It felt as though Elzeth had been punched out of Tomas, leaving him empty and all too human.

It wasn't true. He could still feel Elzeth within, writhing in his own agony. But the connection that made Tomas a host had been burned away, leaving nothing but ashes in its wake. Tomas curled around his stomach, wrapping his arms tightly around his abdomen and willing Elzeth to be unharmed.

He looked up, forcing himself to attend to what remained of the battle.

If there was any consolation, it was that whatever he experienced seemed minor compared to the others. The two knights they'd been fighting were on the ground, spasming with seizures that threatened to snap bones. Myra, thankfully, was unconscious.

If he could only get to his feet, he could end this battle now. He tried rising, but fell back to his knees as his lower back spasmed. He tried again, but failed even worse. His body was done.

That was when the other knights appeared, pouring out of the building that had reminded Tomas of barracks. Six of them charged toward the battlefield, looking to do to Tomas what he'd imagined doing to the host-knights they'd just been fighting.

Tomas swore and tried to stand, but his legs wobbled and collapsed under him. For a moment, he contemplated just lying there and waiting for the end.

Alas, he didn't think the knights would be terribly honorable about it. He'd never been too popular with them.

A familiar fire burned in his belly, and the connections he'd thought were burned away flared back to life. Out of the ashes, Elzeth rose and returned to Tomas. Strength flooded tired limbs and Tomas pushed himself to his feet.

"Good to have you back, friend," he said.

"Let's not do that again," Elzeth replied.

"Agreed."

His choice galled him, no matter how obvious it was. He sheathed his sword and ran toward Myra. Against six knights, after what he'd just been through, he had no chance. And if that weapon fired again, he'd be as helpless as a newborn foal. He scooped Myra up and threw her over his shoulder, then he turned and ran, Elzeth burning bright once again. Tomas knew when this was over, he'd suffer for days, but that would be a problem he'd welcome if he survived.

To his surprise, the knights didn't pursue. They reached the host-knights and stopped, forming a defensive perimeter while the host-knights recovered. Tomas gave the area one last look before he turned the corner and disappeared from view.

He ran north through the streets, hoping to rendezvous with the 34th. If they were going to take the weapon, they would need to do it together.

A few houses later, Myra coughed and swore. "Put me down."

Tomas did, then reached out to catch her as she wobbled on her feet. She swatted his aid away, then bent over and vomited. She wiped the back of her hand across her face when she was done. "That was a lot worse than last time."

"Yeah. You good to move?"

"One moment." She dry-heaved one last time, then stood up straight. "That's better. What's the plan?"

"Return to the 34th. Assault the weapon again with help and see if we can find the others."

"Good plan."

"Thanks." Tomas led them north, but they didn't move fast. There were more rifles firing than before, and it didn't take long for Tomas to figure out why. They came across one of the major thoroughfares and found a battle that stretched from the wall almost to where they stood.

The street was filled with soldiers, and a glance was more than sufficient to see that Gavan and his troops vastly outnumbered the church forces.

But the church had more guards remaining than Tomas expected, and they were all up on the roofs, raining deadly fire down on the soldiers as small groups of swordsmen waded against the tide of the 34th.

It should have been an impossible battle for the church.

The differences in numbers should have been too great. But the 34th wasn't making the progress Tomas would have expected. "You find Gavan," he ordered Myra. "I'm going to clear some of the roofs and see if I can figure out what's happening."

Myra nodded and ran toward the battlefield. Tomas looked up at the roofs. "Ready?"

"After you." Elzeth flared bright, and Tomas scaled the walls of the nearest house. For the moment, the attention of the rifles was on the slowly advancing 34th, so Tomas mapped out a rough route.

Then he noticed for the first time the cloud rising beyond the wall, unlike anything he'd seen before. From where he stood, he couldn't see the actual land, but the cloud that rose high into the sky was testament enough to the damage that had been done. It billowed out, looking almost like a dark tree that blotted out a fair part of the horizon.

Tomas feared to discover how much of the 34th had been caught in that blast. It went a long way toward explaining their slower-than-expected push into the settlement, though.

He sprinted forward, leaping from roof to roof with ease. The first two rifles he cut down never even knew he was behind them. The third saw him, but too late to react. By the time he reached the fourth, he was starting to attract attention. He shifted directions quickly, but one bullet still grazed his leg.

More rifles turned their attention to their assailant, which was one of the first tactical mistakes Tomas had seen the church guards make. He would have kept firing into the crowd below.

Hopefully, it would be enough. He cut down three more

rifles before dropping into a group of church spears that were effectively holding back a much larger army force. A few moments later, the 34th had broken through and charged farther down the street.

The church's resistance couldn't last much longer. As devastating as the attack from the weapon had been, the 34th still had hundreds of troops.

Tomas found an officer and was given directions to Gavan's location, which allowed Tomas a glimmer of hope. He'd worried that Gavan had been caught by the blast.

A few minutes later, he was safely within one of the houses that had been taken over and used as a command post. Messengers ran back and forth, relaying information at a dizzying speed. But Gavan and his closest aides kept on top of it all, spreading their forces through the settlement and putting an end to the last pockets of resistance.

Gavan saw Tomas and let command shift to some of his officers. Tomas saw the man's eyes were rimmed with red, but he held himself stiffly, and there was a fire in his gaze that hadn't been there before. "Good to see you, Tomas. Myra says you saw the weapon, and we need to take it out. Can you do it?"

"It would be better if you could flatten it with your cannons."

Gavan's voice was tight. "The cannons are gone. Can it be done?"

Tomas swore. "It can be done, but it'll be bloody."

"What do you need?"

"It's guarded by six knights and two host-knights. I need everyone you can spare. Snipers would be welcome if there are any around."

Gavan nodded. "You can take my own honor guard, and we'll see if we can scrounge you up a sniper or two. We don't have too many people to spare, though." Gavan's voice caught for a moment, and Tomas nodded.

"I understand. It'll get done, sir."

Myra interjected. "Sir, why don't we just wait them out? You'll have complete control of the settlement soon, and then can make a more organized attack. You're already here."

Gavan shook his head. "Against another enemy, sure. But no one is allowing themselves to be taken prisoner here. Everyone is fighting to the death. Do you think they'll let the weapon fall into our hands so we can build our own?"

Myra paled as she understood. "That means as soon as they think the town is lost..." Her voice trailed off.

"Exactly. We don't know how often the weapon can fire, but I can't afford to take any chances. Almost everyone I know is in this settlement right now, and I'll be damned if I let the church turn the weapon on them."

All Myra could do was nod. "Then it'll get done, sir."

"Good." Gavan turned back to the command tent. "Because we're all counting on you two now."

34

Tomas felt considerably better having Gavan's honor guard behind him, but it didn't mean he looked forward to the battle to come. The host-knights had already proven to be more than a match for him and Myra, and the other six knights were maybe an even larger problem. Gavan's honor guard would be among the most skilled swords in the 34th, but Tomas didn't know how to rank them against a church knight. He feared they would be found wanting.

Against a more reasonable opponent, he would have argued Myra's case for restraint in the command tent. But from everything he'd seen, and from everything he'd heard from others, the church either planned to win here or die. They would entertain no other solution.

Their passage through the streets of Kimson suffered only the briefest of delays due to fighting. Tomas had broken the back of the resistance on his way to Gavan, and now only the cleaning up and securing of the settlement remained. A few random rifle shots still echoed out, and

Tomas heard the familiar sounds of steel meeting steel once, but the streets were largely quiet.

They reached the moat-like street, only to find all eight knights waiting for their arrival. Tomas considered asking them to step aside, but a single glance at their faces told him he would only be wasting his breath. So he drew his sword and prepared to fight.

"Unity?" he asked Elzeth. Against the host-knights, he saw no other path to victory.

"Suppose so," Elzeth replied, sounded as tired as an old farmer after a long day in the fields, asked to do one last chore by his loving wife. Tomas took a deep breath and burned away the thin veil that separated him and Elzeth.

In the bright light of unity, there was no thought. There was no place for fear, worry, or doubt. Tomas knew only this moment. Despite the violence surrounding him, Tomas felt a deep sense of peace as he transcended the thoughts that typically raced through his mind.

The same host-knight from before met his charge, grinning from ear to ear as his sword carved random patterns in the air. This time, Tomas could follow the man's movements, albeit just barely.

The ferocity of their first exchange cleared the area around them, leaving them to duel alone. Myra and her previous opponent resumed their duel. The six knights met the members of Gavan's honor guard, and the final battle was joined in earnest.

Tomas didn't retreat this time, but he made no progress, either. As before, the knight's relentless attacks prevented Tomas from executing that one clean strike that would change the course of the battle.

Tomas growled at his inability to progress. He pushed himself harder, but there was nothing left to squeeze from

Elzeth. The heat radiating off the knight was incredible, and Tomas suspected the man burned through his sagani at a furious rate. Especially after their last duel, the knight had to be close to the physical limits of his body. But Tomas hadn't found those limits yet, and the host-knight still controlled the battlefield.

On the next pass, when Tomas should have backed up, he flung himself forward, heedless of the danger. The knight's sword came closer to opening Tomas up, but Tomas kept just far enough ahead to prevent his demise. The knight's kick caught him completely off guard, though.

Tomas sprawled in the dirt, coughing up dust. He rose to his feet quickly, noticing the blue glow by his right boot. It called to him and he reached down and picked it up.

As soon as his fingers made contact, it was as if a veil had been torn from his eyes. The world around him was deeper and more mysterious than he'd ever known. A small sun glowed near the heart of Kimson, whispering promises of eternal peace.

That was where he needed to be.

Tomas stepped toward it, only to find his path blocked. The host-knight stood before him, supported by all his peers. The host-knight charged the same as before, but Tomas' perception was as different as night was from day. It was as if he walked two worlds at once. One was the physical plane he was well familiar with, but the other was the world of the nexuses and the sagani.

He assumed the knight moved as fast as ever. The sagani within him burned even brighter than the nexus at the heart of Kimson, consumed by the knight's fervor. But Tomas saw differently. His senses were painfully sharp, his mind and body impossibly quick. He brought both hands to his sword, pressing the shard between his hand and the hilt. He would never let it go.

Tomas drifted forward, finally agile enough to slip through the host-knight's assault. He cut the knight twice, but the man never retreated. The knight's sagani roared, and Tomas heard it as clearly as if it were Elzeth. One final cut finished the fight, and Tomas felt a tug as the sagani within the knight winked out of existence.

The death of the host-knight was the small pebble that unbalanced the scale of the battle. Free from interference, Tomas attacked the other host-knight. Focused as he was on Myra, he had no chance.

Then Tomas turned to the heart of Kimson, the nexus the settlement had been built over. He strode toward it, even as the remaining knights fought to intercept him. But they were already occupied with Gavan's honor guard. Tomas cut down those that came too close, their skill not nearly sufficient. His quiet rampage freed up the soldiers of the 34th, and they soon overpowered the remaining knights.

Tomas was halfway to the arena when the screams echoed once again. This time they had a different pitch, and he imagined he was caught in an endless hallway with the agonized voices.

In one world, he saw nothing. The sun beat down on Kimson, an early promise of the summer to come. Nothing in sight moved, and the only sound was the footsteps of Gavan's honor guard following behind him.

But in the other world, the space around them warped, almost as though he was moving through a tunnel. The air around him seemed emptier.

Too late, he intuited the mechanism of the weapon. He turned around to yell at the others, but the tunnel was too wide. It would engulf them all, no matter how fast they ran.

Even with all the strength the nexus gave him, he couldn't escape.

Thanks to his second sight, Tomas saw the destruction coming. The screaming crescendoed, reaching a pitch that made Tomas want to cover his ears. An enormous amount of energy ran along the thread that connected the heart of Kimson to the enormous power deep beneath Tomas' boots. It filled the heart and was focused by something Tomas couldn't discern. Then the lens turned its terrible eye on him.

The power erupted from the weapon, and Tomas saw it all. It originated in a spot directly above the arena. He saw the flash of light as the energy blasted away from the focal point, and watched in fascination as the ground in front of him simply vanished. On the physical plane, there was little to see except for a distorted wave in the air.

The true power of the attack was only apparent thanks to unity and his connection with the shard. Energy filled the tunnel and poured down it like a flood of water dumped down a pipe. It barreled toward them, and there was nothing they could do to avoid it.

Tomas raised his sword in defiance and waited for the end.

Then the wave of power hit him.

35

———

Tomas was in a clearing, walking around on all fours with a familiarity he'd never known. He was surrounded by sagani, and he felt a powerful sense of belonging, like he'd just come home after a long trip. Knowledge passed between them, not as words, but as sensations, as memory.

Stories of the creatures to the east, new arrivals to the land but with a power unlike anything the sagani had observed before. One sagani, who took the form of an old bear, shared with them a not-memory, a memory of what might be.

It was a skill they all possessed, to create these memories of possible futures. But the old bear was by far the most practiced. The new creatures were here, and had an affinity for the hearts. In the old bear's not-memory, the creatures expanded and explored, as though it were a compulsion. They meddled with forces they did not understand, forces they had no memory of.

A series of events passed through Tomas, finally carrying language with the memory. He was in a city, bigger than any he'd been in since childhood. The buildings were of an old style, yet new. The memory had familiar contours, but the name of the place eluded him. He walked down the street, greeting passersby who seemed pleased to see him.

Then he was in a battle, fighting with an unfamiliar sword as archers rained down arrows. Bloody and near death, three arrows jutting from his chest, he reached out to the familiar pale blue glow of the nexus.

The old bear stood before him again, sharing memories and not-memories with ease. A command to return.

Then he was she, advising a general as to the best course of action. Sounds of battle echoed from far away. Later, as an older woman, she found a nexus and embraced it.

The old bear appeared again.

Then he was fighting yet again in the middle of a battlefield Tomas remembered. Tomas felt a tremendous pain, and then all was quiet. In his last vision, he stared at his own face, the same one he had looked at in the mirror for years.

Tomas gasped, and he was once again in Kimson. His whole body burned, as though someone had stacked kindling and lit a bonfire in his chest. Tomas wheezed, desperate for air and unable to find any. Before him, a wide line of destruction stretched from just beyond the arena to directly underneath his hands and his outstretched sword.

He looked back to see a collection of wide-eyed members of Gavan's honor guard. Myra stood among them, the same expression on her face. He looked down, and with his second sight, he saw the weaponized energy traveling down the thread that connected the shard in his hand to the heart of the planet. What the church had taken, he had returned.

The tunnel around him was gone and the air was full of dust.

There were no real thoughts in unity, but his emotions were sharper. He was glad the others were alive, and whenever he looked at the arena, his blood began to boil. He ran toward the odd building, following the path of the recently destroyed ground. It was as if they had rolled out a welcoming mat just for him.

Shots rang out from the arena, but the snipers who were part of Gavan's contingent made short work of the last guards.

Tomas felt the air changing once again as the weapon began its preparations to fire, but then he was at the arena walls. He clambered up the side, then froze at the sight when he reached the top.

Because it looked like an arena from the outside, he had assumed that it would look like an arena on the inside. He couldn't have been more wrong. There were no stands here, no place for observers to watch a contest. The walls were just as vertical on the other side, and the interior was a mess of wires and metal machinery Tomas couldn't begin to guess at.

Off to one side he saw cages, tall enough for one person to stand in. He saw Hardin and Emerson in the cages, but no sign of Kyle. Another structure was near the center of the arena, made completely of metal. Hardin, spotting him on the wall, gestured in that direction.

Tomas dropped and landed among the maze of machinery. Steam hissed to his left, and gears clanked behind him. He ran through the twisted passages even as the air around him grew emptier. He looked around, but saw no evidence of a tunnel to focus the power. The screams began once again, louder than he'd ever heard them. This time, they began at the same volume they'd crescendoed at earlier.

He ran as fast as he could, reaching the central metal structure just as the screams began to reach their peak. The entrance was guarded by two church guards, who drew swords and prepared to fight. Against Tomas, deep in unity, there was nothing they could do. He walked through them, cutting them down before they could even get close.

Tomas stepped into the chamber and once again froze. It was lit from above with a bright white light that reminded him of those strange lights under a mountain, long ago. The cardinal was there, along with what appeared to be two assistants. He stood by a large machine, his eyes focused on a gauge.

But none of that was what drew Tomas' attention.

He had found Kyle. The host was naked and chained to a metal X. He looked gaunt and sickly, and Tomas guessed he had lost nearly a third of his mass. Beside Kyle stood a knight, standing next to two waist-high pillars that he rested his hands on. Tomas saw the sagani within the knight, too.

Tomas turned his attention first to the knight. He launched himself at the man, who stood as still as the pillars he held onto. His eyes were open, but they were focused somewhere far away. The assistants tried to stop Tomas, but he slid around them without problem.

Behind him, the cardinal spoke. "Too late."

He pushed a button on his machine, and Tomas heard the screams grow to a peak that felt as though a whole furious choir shouted directly into his ear. He watched the power as it was pulled from deep below, an amount even greater than before.

Kyle's screams joined the chorus and his body arched against the metal as the power rushed toward him.

Tomas understood the shape of the machine now. He took another step toward the knight and thrust his sword out. The knight didn't attempt to dodge, and Tomas pierced him straight through the heart.

But the cardinal was right. Tomas had arrived a moment too late. The power possessed a conduit through Kyle, and it gathered at a focal point above the arena. Tomas saw it through his sagani-aided vision, but noticed the light coming through the entrance was brightening, too.

The cardinal laughed, but Tomas barely heard him.

His focus was on the power above. If the knight had been here, it would have had a direction, a purpose. Tomas reached for the pillars, but once again, was too late.

The power erupted, a blinding light and resounding clap turned Tomas' stomach to water. The metal ceiling groaned and crumpled inward as the wave hit it, but the structure otherwise held. Outside, Tomas wondered if anyone else would be so lucky.

Kyle slumped against his chains, held up only by the manacles around his wrists.

The cardinal was still laughing when Tomas ran him through, silencing him for good.

36

———

The cardinal's assistants tried to run, but Tomas was at the entrance well before they reached it. His bloodlust was far from satisfied, and his only desire was to kill them where they stood. A voice in the back of his head, barely louder than a whisper, was the only reason he didn't stain his blade with their blood.

He closed his eyes, cutting off his sight of the physical world, but not that of the world of the sagani. Kyle's sagani still lived, though it was barely more than a light and misty blob to Tomas' eye.

That fact was enough to focus Tomas' thoughts, and the first brick in the wall that separated him from Elzeth was replaced.

That lone brick stood alone for an eternity. He was caught in a purgatory, somewhere short of unity but not back to the way he knew he should be. No matter how hard he struggled, though, nothing changed. Whenever he thought another brick might be prepared, it vanished, pulled away by a song he couldn't hear.

The gem.

He pulled his right hand away from the hilt of the sword. The shard was there, coated in his own blood. He put his hand in his pocket and scraped the shard out of his palm.

Then the rebuilding began, the wall returning to the place it had always been.

Tomas returned to himself, and he rolled his neck. Then he met the eyes of the terrified assistants. "Where are the keys?"

He didn't need to elaborate. One of the assistants pulled a full set of keys from his pocket and tossed them to Tomas. Tomas let them fall. "Get out of here," he said. They obeyed.

Tomas didn't care what happened to them. Gavan and his troops controlled the settlement, if anything was left of them. The assistants would most likely be captured if they tried to flee.

He picked up the keys and walked over to Kyle, already feeling the wave of exhaustion that threatened to settle over him. Tomorrow, which it looked like he would see, was going to be a very rough day. He looked forward to suffering through it. For now, he settled for unlocking Kyle's manacles. Before long he had Kyle draped over his shoulder, and together they left the metal structure.

Tomas grunted when he saw what remained. The blast here wasn't nearly as bad as he'd expected. Metal was bent and machinery was broken, but the force had to have been much greater. A question for later, he supposed.

He dragged Kyle toward the cages where he'd found Hardin and Emerson. Once there, he searched for a key on the ring he'd been given and unlocked the cells. Hardin's required more than a fair bit of force to open, as the metal had been twisted by the blast. Hardin himself was bleeding from a head wound, but he didn't seem concerned about it, so Tomas didn't worry.

Once they were out, they all worked together to carry Kyle. Tomas was grateful, his body near the edge of collapse. He could feel that Elzeth wanted his attention, but now wasn't the time.

When they exited the weapon, they stopped at what they saw. The settlement directly around the weapon, including the church, had been leveled. The nearest standing buildings were homes on the other side of the wide street.

Tomas' mind was eased when he saw Myra, running from behind one of those homes, toward them. She shouted with joy and practically tackled Tomas with an embrace. Tomas staggered but kept his feet.

She stepped back. "You look like crap."

"Rough day."

Myra looked around and the smile on her face faded. She nodded. "Yeah. It really was."

The next morning Tomas watched the others as they loaded Kyle onto a cart. The young host didn't look much better than he had the day before, but he was alive and that was something. Kyle whispered something to Hardin, who came over to Tomas. "Kid wants to talk to you. He's only coherent sometimes, so I hope it lasts."

Tomas nodded, then went over to Kyle. "How you feeling?"

Kyle let out a throaty chuckle. "Been better. Dying doesn't feel too great, if I'm being honest."

Tomas' first instinct was to throw out some sort of meaningless lie, to tell Kyle that it would all work out. But they all knew the truth well enough. "I'll remember you," he said. "Your skill with the bow was extraordinary."

"Thanks. Though to be honest, with the number of rifles coming west, it wouldn't have been long before I was pointless anyway. The place is changing, and I figure it's as good a time as any to take my leave. Just wanted to say thank you for coming for me. That thing is a blasphemy."

Tomas wasn't sure what Kyle expected from him, so he just nodded.

"I know it was a risk for you, coming in for me when I don't have long to live anyway. Just wanted to let you know, it means the world to me to die under an open sky with my friends at my side."

"You're welcome."

Kyle's eyes darted to the side, and Tomas worried he was in the grips of madness. But then he focused again on Tomas. "I also wanted you to know, I saw a lot when they had me hooked to that machine. I don't know if I can make sense of it all, but I think you need to know. There's nothing to fear. You and Elzeth? You're good."

Tomas frowned, and was about to ask Kyle what he meant when the young man's eyes went vacant and he twitched under his blankets. Tomas bowed, then stepped away. "Rest well, friend."

He went over to where the rest of the group was waiting for him. Hardin spoke first. "You sure you want to stay?"

"A deal's a deal. I said I'd never return to either of your settlements, and I won't. But don't worry, I think I can get in touch with Ulva no matter where I am, so I'm sure you'll hear from me soon enough."

Hardin's face scrunched up. "But with *them*?"

"We're all friends for the moment, and I think this is

where I need to be. The army is going to want blood for this, and I mean to help them however I can."

"They're not going to give you your old rank, you know," Myra said.

Tomas smiled. "I was in the unnamed units, so I never had a rank. Nothing to lose there." His smile dropped. "If we do this right, we give the hosts that come after us something to live for. It could mean real peace. And it starts here."

The others had no sarcastic rejoinders to that. Myra stepped up and embraced him. "You take care of yourself."

"You, too. Maybe stay home from now on."

"That's the plan."

Emerson held out his hand, which Tomas took. "Thanks for saving my life," he said.

"Any time."

The others drifted away, leaving Tomas with Hardin. "It's still a damn foolish idea, but after spending the last few weeks with you, I think it might be the most reasonable one I've seen you make."

Tomas chuckled. "Guess we'll see."

"It's been an honor, Tomas. I truly hope we meet again under better circumstances."

"Agreed."

Tomas was surprised when Hardin also wrapped him up in a tight embrace. The giant man nearly squeezed the life out of him.

There was one final round of goodbyes, and then the hosts were gone, leaving Tomas alone with Gavan's surviving soldiers.

∾

Tomas filled his days with as much activity as he could handle, then spent the remainder of his time resting. There was plenty to do. The medical tent always needed volunteers, and Tomas spent a considerable amount of time exploring the remains of the weapon. Engineers spent days studying the machinery, and they frequently turned to Tomas with questions. Slim as his own knowledge was, it was more than anyone else possessed.

Mostly, though, he was avoiding speaking with Elzeth. The knowledge he'd uncovered through the course of the Battle of Kimson was too fresh a revelation, and he wasn't ready to speak calmly about it. From what he felt from Elzeth, the feeling was mutual.

He spent his nights around fires with Gavan's surviving soldiers. Of the original army, barely a fifth remained. But those that survived were bonded together with ties that would never fray. And after everyone heard what Tomas had done, he was welcome wherever he walked.

He couldn't help but compare his time here to Jonasson. In both places, everyone had known who he was and what he was. Even there, though, he hadn't been welcome. Here, he never had to pour his drinks.

The road forward wouldn't be easy, but he wasn't alone.

Finally, on the night of the third day after the battle, Tomas wandered off to the prairie and dropped into the grass to look at the stars. Elzeth stirred uncomfortably in his stomach, then settled. Tomas debated where to start, then figured he'd start with the subject that bothered him only a little less. "So, you've been hosted before."

Elzeth's reply was slow in coming. "Seems that way. The memories feel real, but it's the first time I remembered them."

"But it wasn't surprising to you?" Tomas wanted to keep

the vitriol out of his voice, but he found it nearly impossible. For their whole time together, he'd always assumed it was just the two of them. He imagined his feelings weren't all that different from a spouse who had just found out their partner was having an affair.

"No."

Elzeth didn't say any more, and Tomas wasn't quite sure what to make of the silence. But he didn't want to push too hard, either. He wasn't ready for the answers.

A long quiet stretched between them. Finally, Elzeth brought up the other point. "We need to decide what to do."

"About what?"

"About us."

The answer sent a chill down Tomas' spine. "What do you mean?"

"You feel it as well as I do. We didn't completely break apart from unity. I've lost a part of myself, just like you've lost part of you. We unify again, and I really don't think we're coming back."

He felt the same. Though he felt like himself, the wall between them wasn't complete, not the way it had been. Before, their concerns about unity had been a worry, but now it felt closer to a certainty. "I don't know, Elzeth. I really don't. After all of this, we finally have allies that matter. We're closer than ever to putting a stop to whatever the church is doing. I don't want to lose myself, but if there's a cause that's worth that sacrifice, it's this one."

"Yeah. I know. But I don't like it, and in the heat of the moment, I'm not sure I'd unify. Just so you know."

Tomas watched the stars and waited for his emotions to subside. It was no more than he'd expected. But it still hurt. Though he knew more than ever about Elzeth, he felt farther away than any time since the beginning. "It kind of feels like we're reaching the end of the road, doesn't it, partner?"

"It does."

Tomas swallowed hard. "Together?"

There was another long pause, as Elzeth considered his answer carefully.

"Always."

THE ADVENTURES CONTINUE!

Top o' the morning!

I hope that wherever you are in the world, and whenever it is you're reading this, that you're doing well.

First, as an author, let me thank you for reading *Frontier's End*. Whether this is the first book of mine you've read or my twentieth, I hope that you enjoyed it. There have never been more ways to be entertained, and it truly means the world to me that you choose to spend your time in these pages.

If you enjoyed the story, rest assured the Tomas' and Elzeth's next adventure isn't far off. Keep an eye out for the next book, releasing soon!

And if you're looking to spread the word, there's few better ways to support the story by leaving a review where you purchased the book!

Thanks again!

Ryan

STAY IN TOUCH

Thanks once again for reading *Frontier's End*. I had a tremendous amount of fun writing this story, and am looking forward to writing more of Tomas and Elzeth.

If you enjoyed the story, I'd ask that you consider signing up to get emails from me. You can do so at:

www.waterstonemedia.net/newsletter

I typically email readers once or twice a month, and one of my greatest pleasures over the past five years has been getting to know the people reading my stories.

If I'm being honest, email is my favorite way of communicating with readers. Whether it's hearing from soldiers stationed overseas or grandmothers tending to their gardens, email has allowed me to make new friends all over the world.

Email subscribers also get all the goodies. From free books in all formats, to sample chapters and surprise short stories, if I'm giving something away, it's through email.

I hope you'll join us.

Ryan

ALSO BY RYAN KIRK

Saga of the Broken Gods

Band of Broken Gods

Last Sword in the West

Last Sword in the West

Eyes of the Hidden World

A Sword Named Vengeance

Wraith's Revenge

Frontier's End

Oblivion's Gate

The Gate Beyond Oblivion

The Gates of Memory

The Gate to Redemption

Relentless

Relentless Souls

Heart of Defiance

Their Spirit Unbroken

The Nightblade Series

Nightblade

World's Edge

The Wind and the Void

Blades of the Fallen

Nightblade's Vengeance

Nightblade's Honor

Nightblade's End

Standalone Novels

Blades of Shadow

The Primal Series

Primal Dawn

Primal Darkness

Primal Destiny

ABOUT THE AUTHOR

Ryan Kirk is the bestselling author of the *Nightblade* series of books. When he isn't writing, you can probably find him playing disc golf or hiking through the woods.

www.waterstonemedia.net
contact@waterstonemedia.net

 facebook.com/waterstonemedia
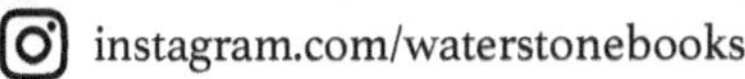 twitter.com/waterstonebooks
instagram.com/waterstonebooks

www.ingramcontent.com/pod-product-compliance
Lightning Source LLC
Chambersburg PA
CBHW050847190726
48286CB00007B/2262